D1433716

THE WILD MARAUDER

THE WILD MARAUDER

Ann Barker

CHIVERS
THORNDIKE

This Large Print book is published by BBC Audiobooks Ltd, Bath, England and by Thorndike Press®, Waterville, Maine, USA.

Published in 2005 in the U.K. by arrangement with Robert Hale Limited.

Published in 2005 in the U.S. by arrangement with Robert Hale Limited.

U.K. Hardcover   ISBN 1–4056–3109–0 (Chivers Large Print)
U.K. Softcover   ISBN 1–4056–3110–4 (Camden Large Print)
U.S. Softcover   ISBN 0–7862–6983–9 (General)

The text of this Large Print edition is unabridged.
Other aspects of the book may vary from the original edition.

Set in 16 pt. New Times Roman.

Printed in Great Britain on acid-free paper.

British Library Cataloguing in Publication Data available

Library of Congress Control Number: 2004110550

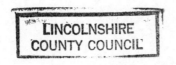

For Sally, of whom I am very proud.

CHAPTER ONE

'Nella, Charlie is here! I heard his voice in the hall! Do you suppose that he has come to ask for my hand?'

Fenella Parrish looked at her older sister Dora. Her eyes were shining with hope and her mouth was curved in a shy smile.

'Oh Dora, I don't know,' replied Fenella. 'But I shouldn't be surprised.' It was on the tip of her tongue to add that it would be about time, considering for how long Dora had been waiting, but to say this would scarcely have been tactful. The fact that Charles Edwin Crossfield, third Earl of Yelden, and Miss Dora Parrish, elder daughter of Sir Humphrey and Lady Parrish, were made for each other was something that had been known by half the county for the last five years at least. Nor should it be supposed that his lordship— known to all for as long as anyone could remember as Charlie—had failed to propose because the bride of his choice did not meet with his family's approval. This was quite the opposite of the truth. Miss Parrish, with a fortune of £5000, some quite justifiable pretensions to beauty, and a manner as engaging as her appearance, had been judged to be ideal future countess material by both of Charlie's parents. Sadly, Lady Yelden had died three years ago, and had never had the chance to see her hopes fulfilled. Her husband, however, had encouraged his son to press his suit, and as a consequence, Charlie had been on the brink of proposing twelve months before.

Unfortunately, no sooner was his decision made than his father, though apparently hale and hearty, died most unexpectedly of a heart attack. Charlie was his parents' only child, so all the responsibility for the estate fell upon his shoulders. This, and a necessary period of mourning, had inevitably engaged his attention for some time for the past few months, matters of business had taken him to London, and kept him there.

Only that morning, however, news had arrived via the carter, who visited both Yelden Hall and Brightstones, where the Parrishes lived, that Charlie was home, and that he had brought with him some visitors from London. Now, it appeared that Charlie had arrived at Brightstones at last, and not even the most confirmed pessimist could have declared that there was no chance of a proposal that day.

Miss Fenella Parrish, at eighteen, two years younger than her sister, was not a pessimist, but she was something of a romantic, and it had occurred to her more than once that Charlie might have rushed to her sister's side rather more expeditiously, no matter what his circumstances. After all, there was no doubt that Dora was by far the prettiest girl in the county. Not even her relations could have been accused of partiality for saying so. Her raven curls, clear complexion and dreamy blue eyes had long since lured a steady stream of beaux to her door. Had she wished, she could have had her pick, but she had remained committed to Charlie, and that, Fenella decided with a small sigh as she helped her sister to arrange her hair more becomingly, was half the trouble. Charlie had grown to take the patient, sweet-natured Dora for granted.

'It would serve him right if you kept him waiting another half an hour,' said Fenella, giving voice to a piece of advice without revealing her reasoning behind it. 'It's not good for gentlemen to think that we are always at their beck and call.'

Dora laughed out loud. 'And where did you learn that piece of wisdom?' she asked. 'Nella, there is no question of that sort of play-acting between Charlie and me. We *know* that we are intended for each other.' Fenella had not heard Dora laugh like that in a long time. She hoped that Charlie's level of commitment to the match was as great as her sister's.

Since Dora herself would not delay, Fenella made her own preparations last for as long as possible, until at last Dora said, as impatiently as one of her sweet nature could, 'O come *on*, Nella! You know I can't go downstairs without you, and I want to see Charlie.'

They hurried downstairs, Dora setting the pace.

'Where are we to go, Berry?' Dora asked the butler, who had worked at Brightstones all their lives.

'The saloon, Miss Dora,' he replied.

'What, both of us?' Fenella exclaimed involuntarily. Berry permitted himself a small fatherly smile.

'I believe so, Miss Fenella.' The sisters looked at one another, then entered the room indicated.

The room had more occupants than they had expected. Instead of just finding their mother and father entertaining Lord Yelden, they were confronted by the sight of three other persons, one gentleman and two ladies, all dressed in the height of fashion, as was Charlie himself.

Fenella was a little afraid that her open-hearted sister might hurry forward and greet Charlie without any regard for the dictates of propriety, but she did not do so. It might be that the sensation of being face to face with a fashionable London gentleman played some part in restraining her; for the Charlie who came towards them to make his bow was somewhat different from the young man they had always known.

Charlie had never been neglectful of his appearance, but now he had acquired an unmistakable London gloss. When he had gone to London, he had still worn his own hair. Now, he sported an immaculate wig, and his russet brocade coat fitted him like a glove. To Dora, it seemed as if she was meeting an elegant stranger for the first time.

But when Charlie came towards her, he bowed and smiled, and in that smile, she recognized the boy with whom she had played, and the young man with whom she had fallen in love.

'Dora, my dear, you look as lovely as ever,' he declared in a fashionable drawl.

Dora smiled back at him. 'And you, Charlie, look very elegant,' she replied. 'I would hardly have recognized you.'

Charlie turned to Fenella. 'Fenella, I do believe you've grown an inch.'

'All the better, then,' replied Fenella. 'You'll find it harder, now, to put a frog down my back.'

Charlie laughed and begged leave to introduce his London friends, Mr Stephen Maxfield, and his wife and sister. His wife was a petite brunette, with lively hazel eyes and an outgoing flirtatious manner. Miss Maxfield seemed quieter, with a fair complexion and light-brown hair.

'We have come on a special mission today,' Charlie said, when the introductions had been made. 'My guests have prevailed upon me to organize a ball while they are here, so I have been to Bel and the Dragon in Cookham and fixed it for next Friday. I do hope that you will all be free.'

Dora seemed to be unable to find a reply, so Fenella looked at her mother and said, 'Mama?'

'Why certainly,' declared Lady Parrish. 'What a delightful scheme! We shall all consider ourselves engaged, shall we not, my dear?'

'What? Oh, oh yes, of course,' replied her spouse, when thus appealed to. He much preferred riding about his acres, hobnobbing with his tenants, or even, of an evening, sitting quietly with a book, to doing the pretty at social events.

'I must say, it is delightful to meet you all at last,' said Mrs Maxfield, in lively tones. 'I cannot recall how often Charlie has said to us how much he values the friendship of the Parrish family.'

'Charlie is very kind,' said Dora. Only her close friends and family would have been able to tell that she was rather more subdued than normal. 'We value his friendship too.'

'Then we must all be friends as well,' declared the vivacious Mrs Maxfield. 'Any friend of Charlie's is a friend of ours. I cannot tell you at how many functions he has said how much he wished that his dear friends the Parrishes were there.'

This conversation, which seemed to indicate a lively social life in London, as opposed to a

6

life dominated by business matters, clearly left Dora rather subdued. Fenella was glad, therefore, that before the party from Yelden Hall left, Charlie took the opportunity of taking her older sister on one side, and having some confidential conversation with her.

After the visitors had gone, with Sir Humphrey escorting them to their carriage, Lady Parrish made much of the promised treat.

'I do not know precisely why it may be, but it is some time since a ball was given in this area,' she said. 'It will be a good opportunity for you both. We must make sure that you are dressed suitably, for I do not want you to be shone down by these London visitors.'

Fenella waited for her sister to speak, but as the silence threatened to lengthen into something rather awkward, she said, 'My bronze gown will do I think, Mama. I have not had it very long, you know.'

Her mother nodded thoughtfully. 'Yes, the over-dress will do very well,' she agreed. 'But I never thought that that white under-dress did very much for it. A new one of cream, with perhaps some gold embroidery, would be better. We must go into Maidenhead tomorrow, and look for some material to make one. Dora, you must have a completely new gown, I think. It will not do for Charlie to see you looking anything other than your best.'

Dora had begun to recover her complexion,

but at these words, she opened her mouth, closed it again, burst into tears, and ran from the room. Lady Parrish looked at her younger daughter in consternation.

'Oh dear,' she murmured. 'What has happened to upset her now?'

'I think that perhaps Dora had been hoping that Charlie would come to see her on his own,' replied Fenella. 'It was a shock for her to see him with those fashionable people.' And especially those fashionable women, she added to herself silently.

'Well no doubt he will in time,' replied her mother. 'But I expect he felt that it would be impolite to be riding about the countryside and deserting the people he has brought with him to Yelden Hall.' She sighed briefly. 'It would be foolish to suppose that Charlie has not met with any temptations whilst he has been in London. The attachment between him and Dora is of long standing, of course. But she must make sure that she looks her very best for this ball. It will never do for her to start taking Charlie for granted.'

Repressing the urge to say that as far as she was concerned the boot was on the other foot, Fenella merely said, 'I'll go after her. It may be that after I've calmed her down, I'll be able to give her thoughts a new direction by talking about shopping for a new gown.'

'You're a good girl,' said Lady Parrish, getting up and patting her fondly on the arm.

'Don't think that I forget about you. When Dora and Charlie are safely married, it will be *your* turn, for I know that your sister will be delighted to bring you out.'

'Thank you, Mama,' said Fenella, before hurrying upstairs. Dora was where Fenella had expected to find her, lying down on her bed, her face turned away from the door. This was where Dora always came when she needed solace. Fenella sat down on the bed next to her sister and waited. She knew that Dora would not talk until she was ready. Sure enough, after a very few minutes, she rolled over to face her sister, a sure sign that she was prepared to communicate.

'What is it, Dora?' asked Fenella. 'Did Charlie say something to upset you?' Dora sniffed, and Fenella handed her a handkerchief which lay on the bedside table, and which had obviously already been well used for mopping up tears.

'He didn't mean to,' replied Dora in pathetic tones. 'He just asked me to . . .' Her voice died away.

'Well?'

'He said that Miss Maxfield would feel a little strange away from London, and asked for my kindness on her behalf,' said Dora.

'What is there to take exception to in that?' asked Fenella. 'She looked like a quiet little mouse to me. I don't suppose she has many friends.'

9

'Yes, but . . .' Again Dora fell silent, pulling her handkerchief between her hands this time.

'But what?'

'I can't help but wonder why he thinks I should be so particularly kind to her,' said Dora all of a rush. 'It makes me think that perhaps he might have a . . . a fondness for her.'

Fenella smiled. 'Dora, have you looked in the mirror recently?' Dora looked at her questioningly. One of her most endearing qualities was her utter lack of personal vanity. 'She can't hold a candle to you,' Fenella went on persuasively. 'I'm sure she has many good qualities, but she's not half as pretty as you are, and she cannot possibly have a better nature.'

Dora could not help laughing then. It was a tiny, pathetic sound, but at least it was a laugh of a sort.

'Nella, you'll make me big-headed,' she said.

'Impossible,' replied Fenella. 'I've never met anyone with so little natural conceit. In any case, he may just be telling you the simple truth. Mrs Maxfield looks a very confident, out-going person, and probably she is inclined to cast her sister-in-law into the shade. I expect he is just being kind.'

Dora started to look a little more hopeful. 'Oh do you really think so?' she asked.

'Yes, I do. But listen, Dora,' Fenella went on. 'There's no doubt that Charlie will have seen some very attractive ladies in London. He could not help but do so, unless he went round with his eyes shut. You must make sure that you look your very best for the ball to remind him of what he has been missing. Look dazzling on that evening, and show him that perhaps other men are vying for your attentions, and I guarantee that he will propose within a few days. Remember, faint heart never won fine gentleman!'

Dora laughed again, and this time it was a much stronger, more confident sound.

'You're right, Nella,' she said. 'When does Mama want to go shopping? You must help me go through my wardrobe at once, to see if anything can be refurbished. There is no time to lose!'

CHAPTER TWO

After Dora had gone in search of Mama to ask her advice about shoes, Fenella took the chance to slip downstairs and go outside. Dora did her thinking on her bed, but at disturbing times, Fenella always climbed the wall of the old folly.

It had never had any practical function, but had been built specifically as a folly by Fenella's grandfather in his youth and the walls, which looked as if they were crumbling away, were in fact very steady. From her position on the top of the wall, Fenella could see over the perimeter wall into the lane, and if she looked in the opposite direction, she could just see the house through the trees. Naturally, it was a good thing not to have the house in full view, for Mama would take a very dim view of her daughter of eighteen climbing walls.

Once perched on the top, she gave Dora's problem some thought. Although she had put the best possible construction on matters for her sister's sake, Fenella had a feeling that the situation was rather more serious than she would have liked.

She thought back to the time when her governess, Miss Thoroughgood, had been engaged to the Reverend Graham Sandys, a curate who served in a church which was two parishes away. They had been engaged for nearly ten years, unable to marry until he could be granted a parish of his own.

Then one day, when Dora was out visiting with Mama, and Fenella, aged sixteen, was having a drawing lesson outside, Mr Sandys appeared quite unexpectedly at the entrance to the garden. He must have been about thirty-five at this time, and Miss Thoroughgood was thirty, and both of them seemed to Fenella to be positively ancient. Furthermore, neither her governess nor the curate had ever appeared to her to be likely participants in a great romance. But after pausing in the gateway, the clergyman came running towards them with great strides, completely regardless of his dignity. On his face was a look of such joy and excitement that Miss Thoroughgood, quite forgetting the presence of her charge, threw herself into his arms and, in the most natural way, raised her face for his kiss.

It transpired that Mr Sandys had just been invited to be the vicar of the next parish and he was therefore now in a position to support Miss Thoroughgood as his wife. He admitted somewhat sheepishly that he had come straight away to break the news to his fiancé, not even stopping to inform his mother, who lived only two doors away from him.

It seemed to Fenella that if a curate could so forget himself as to rush to his beloved's side regardless of any other consideration, then a young man like Charlie, who, with his lithe figure, bright eyes and clear complexion, looked as if he ought to be a figure of romance, could at least make haste to see Dora as soon as he was back in the district. Furthermore, he ought to manage to do it without a crowd of London visitors hanging about his neck.

Nevertheless, he had come; he had brought the visitors, and he had organized a ball, and therein, Fenella truly believed, lay Dora's chance. The chief problem, however, was whether Dora would be able to make the most of that chance. Fenella had not attended many balls, but she knew very well how things worked. Subtle signals were given; the language of the fan; a bow carefully angled to show interest; the holding of a hand for fractionally longer than was necessary; all valuable weapons in the art of flirtation.

Unfortunately, however, Dora was not very good at flirting. All the young men who would gladly have taken Charlie's place were much too earnest to do such a thing, and furthermore, their feelings could really be hurt if Dora only flirted with them to get Charlie's attention. This was especially true of Dudley. Fenella sighed a little when she thought about Dudley Sampson. He was so very handsome, and there had been a time when she had been very taken with him. But he had never looked her way, being entirely captivated by Dora, and in the end, Fenella had resigned herself to just being his friend.

No, Dudley would never flirt with Dora. His feelings would show too clearly, and Dora would hate to hurt him. But something must be done to make Charlie realize what he was missing.

Fenella climbed down from her wall, without having found an answer to this problem. She walked back to the house thoughtfully. She was not going to give up until she had found some way of helping her sister.

With barely a week to go to the promised

14

ball, the Parrish ladies were kept very busy. A visit to Maidenhead the following day resulted in the purchase of material for a new cream petticoat for Fenella. It had just the kind of gold embroidery on it which Lady Parrish had envisaged, and would go very well with her bronze gown.

All three ladies were somehow aware that this ball would prove to be a significant occasion for Dora, so she was to have a completely new gown of blue taffeta with a blue and silver petticoat.

Any women of the household who could sew were pressed into service. When the day of the ball arrived, therefore, even the little kitchen maid—who had proved to be surprisingly adept with a needle—was able to say that she had had a hand in the fashioning of Miss Dora's gown.

That afternoon, before it was time to get ready, Fenella escaped to her favourite thinking place. She had not yet arrived at a solution to the problem, and although Dora would undoubtedly be the prettiest young lady at the ball, she could easily ruin everything by being too welcoming and too eager. What was to be done?

She was roused from her mood of abstraction by the sound of a horse's hooves. Looking down, she discovered that she was an object of rather amused speculation for the gentleman who was seated upon the same

15

horse. He inclined his head to her, a polite gesture which was slightly at variance with his wry grin, and he said in a voice which was firm, clear and rather deep, 'That's a fine perch you have there, ma'am.'

She should not, of course, have any conversation with a strange gentleman without an introduction. On the other hand, she should not be sitting on a wall either, and as was always the case when she was in that particular spot, she felt herself freed from normal conventions.

'Yes, I can see everything,' she replied.

'Aren't you afraid you'll fall?' he asked her.

'Aren't you afraid you'll fall off that horse?' she riposted.

He burst out laughing. It was a full, rich sound. 'I've been riding all my life,' he said, as soon as he was able. Then, before she could reply, he smiled with understanding. 'You've been climbing that wall all your life, haven't you?'

'Very nearly,' she answered nodding.

'Then since you have such a fine vantage point, perhaps you'll be so good as to give me some directions,' he said, changing the subject. 'I appear to have missed my way.'

'Where are you going?' Fenella asked him.

'I'm looking for Yelden Hall,' he replied. 'I was hoping that this might be it, but as there are no daughters living there, I must suppose myself to be mistaken.'

16

Fenella nodded. 'This is Brightstones,' she told him. 'My father, Sir Humphrey Parrish, owns it. But you have not gone so very far wrong, for Yelden Hall is not far distant from here. Are you expected, sir?'

He shook his head. 'I have been told that a cousin of mine is staying there with Lord Yelden, and I rather thought that I would look her up.' He paused, then went on, 'Shall we climb down from our respective eminences and meet at yonder gate so that we can introduce ourselves properly?'

Fenella hesitated briefly, then climbed down. He was clearly a genuine visitor from what he had said, and he would hardly think of insulting her now that he had heard that she was the daughter of a baronet, and on her father's property. She opened the gate in the wall, and found him standing outside, holding his horse's bridle. He was tall, probably about the same height as Charlie, and lean, with broad shoulders. His hair—unlike Charlie, he wore his own—was a very dark brown, with a streak of white running back from one temple to where it was caught rather untidily behind his head with a black ribbon. His face was lean and weatherbeaten, and his eyes were an unusual shade of green, similar to laurel in tone. He was dressed serviceably, rather than fashionably, for riding, and he held his tricorne hat in his hand. At once, it struck Fenella that there was a swashbuckling air to him, as if he

17

went his own way, and be damned to everyone else.

'Come in, sir,' she said. He did so, then bowed politely.

'Giles Beville at your service, ma'am,' he said.

She curtsied in reply. 'I am Fenella Parrish,' she answered. 'We—my sister and I—have known Charlie—I mean, Lord Yelden—all our lives.'

'I have only met him once, briefly,' answered Beville. 'I suppose I'm presuming a little in descending upon him, but as I have said already, my cousin is staying there. I don't know whether you have met her? Constance Maxfield?'

'Mrs Maxfield!' exclaimed Fenella. 'She has been here to visit us! How strange it would have been had you arrived when she was here.'

'Strange indeed,' he murmured. 'You must tell me what you thought of her.'

'Why, I . . . that is, she seemed very agreeable . . . very pleasant,' replied Fenella, rather embarrassed at being asked such a question.

Seeing her confusion he said, 'I'm sorry. That was unfair of me. My only excuse is that I'm genuinely curious. I haven't seen her myself for, oh, five years? Yes, I think it must be five.'

'Good gracious!' exclaimed Fenella, thinking of her own close family. 'How odd!'

'Not really,' he answered. 'I've been abroad for nearly that length of time, you see.' Whilst they were talking, they had wandered over to a low wall which formed part of the folly, and sat down.

'I suppose you will be going to the ball,' Fenella remarked.

'Until I know to which ball you refer, I can't say,' replied Beville. His horse, its reins drawn over its head, stood cropping the grass nearby, and showed no signs of straying. 'Is it to take place at Yelden Hall?'

Fenella shook her head. 'It has been arranged by Charlie in honour of his visitors from London, among them your cousin,' she explained. 'But it is to be held at Bel and the Dragon in Cookham this very evening.'

'That's unfortunate,' he murmured.

'Unfortunate?'

'I happen to have made arrangements to stay there tonight, you see. But I've been riding all day, and I'm rather weary. What I really fancied was a pipe by the fire and a bottle of claret. But now that I have met you and you have told me about it, I can hardly plead ignorance if, when she meets me, my cousin taxes me with my non-appearance, can I?'

'You could always pretend that you hadn't seen me and didn't know about it,' Fenella said demurely. 'I wouldn't give you away.'

He looked at her thoughtfully. 'Egad, I

19

believe you wouldn't,' he said. 'But I can hardly deny all knowledge of it when it's going on in the same building.'

They sat in silence for a short time until, struck by a sudden thought, Fenella said, whilst looking down at her feet, 'If you *should* decide to go, perhaps you would do me a favour.' He was silent. 'It would only be a *very* small favour. Quite a pleasant thing to do, really. But it would make all the difference to someone.'

He gave a small sigh. 'Very well,' he said. 'Tell me what it is, and I'll see if I can do it, but remember that I make no promises.' He waited for her to toss her head and upbraid him for his lack of gallantry, as nearly every woman of his acquaintance would have done.

Instead, she looked down again, then straight up at him, and said frankly, 'It is not for myself, but for my sister, you see. She and Charlie have been in love for years, and should have been betrothed, perhaps even married by now. But Charlie's father died and then there was so much for him to do in London. We all thought that he would come back quite quickly, but he has been in London for rather a long time, and now . . . well . . .'

'You suspect that Lord Yelden's eye might perhaps have strayed to pastures new?' he suggested.

'No, not that precisely,' Fenella answered slowly. 'But he might perhaps have become

20

forgetful of Dora and rather distracted, and I'm sure that he is taking her for granted. I want him to see what he is missing, and turn to her again.'

He looked at her thoughtfully for a moment. 'Forgive me, but has it occurred to you that you might be doing your sister a disservice if you succeed in your object?' he asked her. 'If Yelden has proved to be dilatory in his attentions now, might it not be a sign that it is time for them both to outgrow a youthful attachment, as indeed many do?'

She thought she heard a touch of bitterness in his voice, but when she looked up at him, a little startled, his expression was the same as before.

'Oh no, I don't think it,' replied Fenella earnestly. 'Deep down, Charlie is the same person that he always was. It is just that the delights of London dazzled him, and of course, he could always be sure that Dora would be here, patiently waiting, because that is what Dora does.'

'But not what Miss Fenella Parrish would do in such circumstances, I fancy,' the gentleman hazarded.

Her eyes twinkled. 'Well, I can be very patient if patience is necessary,' she said. 'But if I were Dora, I wouldn't let Charlie go without a fight.'

'A very pardonable sentiment,' answered Beville, smiling too. 'But you are not in the

21

case, are you?'

'No, but I think I know how to do the thing,' she said eagerly. Then she added hesitatingly, 'But only if some gentleman will help.'

'I think I know what's coming,' Beville murmured resignedly.

'I want you to flirt with Dora at the ball, and show Charlie that other men find her attractive,' said Fenella confidingly. 'To be sure, it's a pity that . . .' She stopped, blushing scarlet.

'. . . That I'm not a little more handsome and dashing?' put in Beville.

'Oh no, no!' exclaimed Fenella, hastily. 'Of course you cannot be blamed for your appearance! It is just that Charlie is so fashionable, that . . .' Suddenly realizing the infelicitous nature of her remarks she broke off and looked at him with an expression of dismay. 'Oh dear,' she whispered.

He laughed. 'I appear to be a terrible disappointment all round. Well, I'll just have to do my poor best, won't I?'

'You'll help? Oh, thank you!' exclaimed Fenella, squeezing the gentleman's arm. Then she remembered that she had only just met him, coloured again, and quickly let go of him. He patted her hand paternally, but in his eyes, though she did not see it, was a gleam which was very far from being paternal.

'Yes, I'll help. As I've already told you, my cousin doesn't know that I'm coming to see her, and I don't want you to say anything to her, or indeed to anyone. Let my entrance be a surprise.'

'But Dora . . .' Fenella protested.

'Not even to Dora,' he insisted.

'But can I say that if a gentleman should want to flirt with her then she must respond? Believe me, my sister is not naturally flirtatious.'

He sighed. 'All right, you can say that, but no more. You may not credit it, but I do know how to make an entrance, and I might surprise you. By the way, since we have become conspirators together, you may call me Bev; everyone does.'

Fenella wrinkled her nose. 'Wouldn't that be improper?' she asked him.

'And this conversation isn't?' he replied, raising his brows.

She blushed. 'You are very right. I should never have entered into it.'

'That's stolen my thunder,' he remarked. 'I was to blame for any impropriety.'

'Because you are so much older than I?' she asked, unable to resist glancing up at him through her lashes.

'Because I am more well-versed in worldly matters, you baggage,' he replied.

In his eyes, she seemed to read a message that spoke of foreign lands, strange customs, and adventures far outside the range of her experience.

23

She blushed, rendered suddenly shy. 'I must go and get changed for the ball. I will see you later,' she said. She turned to run across the grass, but she had not taken more than three steps before she turned to face him once more. 'Turn right out of the gate then right again at the bottom of the hill. That will take you to Cookham. Bel and the Dragon is in the high street.' She turned again, and ran in the direction of the house, her skirts flying. Bev stood watching her for a few moments, then led his horse out through the gate, mounted it and set off towards Cookham.

That young woman intrigued him, he decided as he rode, sitting easily in the saddle in the manner of one who has ridden for many weary miles. He had left London five years ago, thoroughly tired of the intrigue and deceit that seemed to be so much a part of life there. He had fled to the Continent only to find that life in Paris, Vienna and Rome was much the same. Here, however, on the top of a folly wall, he had found a freshness and a vitality that surprised him, and the only intrigue in which she seemed to be concerned was for the sake of her sister. Bev laughed. He would play his part to the hilt. That at least would please his valet, who had begun to despair of him recently. His only regret was that he was now bound to flirt outrageously with one sister, when all his instincts urged him to pursue the other. Perhaps it was as well, however. Bitter experience told him that even such as Fenella would inevitably prove to be a disappointment in the end.

CHAPTER THREE

Fenella arrived back at the house to discover that panic had set in.

'Fenella, child!' scolded her mother. 'Wherever have you been? A bare hour is left before we are to set out! You'll never be ready in time! And look at your stockings! What on earth have you been doing?'

'Don't worry, Mother,' said Fenella, wisely ignoring the question in the last part of her mother's speech. 'Millie has laid out everything ready for me.'

'Then hurry and make a start,' said her mother, shooing her upstairs. 'Dora is nearly ready and your papa is pacing up and down.'

'Only at the very idea of having to go at all, I expect,' replied Fenella matter-of-factly.

Just before Lady Parrish was able to declare that they would all be late, Millie pronounced Fenella to be ready and, as she descended the stairs, her mother's harassed expression changed to one of fondest pride.

'Oh Nella, my dear, I vow I have never seen you look so fine!'

Fenella smiled, for she knew that she was

looking her best, but she said merely, 'I shan't be able to hold a candle to Dora.'

Sir Humphrey came into the hall at that moment. He was a handsome, well-built man, dressed this evening in a dark-blue satin coat, but looking, to those who knew him, as if he would be much more comfortable in his riding dress.

'By Jove!' he declared, knowing his duty. 'With three lovely ladies to escort, I shall be quite at a loss as to which two I should offer my arm!' His lady reproved him for his foolishness, but Dora and Fenella smiled at one another as they observed their mother preening discreetly as she passed the mirror above the fireplace.

The day had been a mild one, and it was agreeably exciting to be bowling along on a July evening to attend such an event. Before they left, Fenella had managed to have a private word with her sister.

'Listen Dora,' she had said urgently. 'You must show Charlie that you are not just going to drop into his hands like a ripe apple. Flirt with someone!'

'With whom?' Dora had asked. 'With one of the boys I have known all my life? They would just think I was being silly, or take it seriously and be hurt. In any case, I'm not very good at it.'

'But there might be some strangers from London,' Fenella suggested. 'Friends of

Charlie's perhaps. *They* would not take it seriously. Promise me that if someone wants to flirt with you, then you'll try at least.'

'But Charlie—'

'Charlie will not think any the less of you if he sees that you are attractive to other men. Remember that he is used to London ways, now. Please, Dora, promise me.'

Dora had sighed. 'Very well. If any *strange* gentleman singles me out, then I'll try to respond in kind. But no one will, Nella. Everyone knows that I'm committed to Charlie.'

Fenella smiled to herself. It was very unusual for her to have a secret from her sister and she was rather enjoying this one.

*   *   *

'I thought you'd decided on a quiet evening, sir,' said Forbes, Giles Beville's valet. Together with Rusty, the groom, he had travelled ahead of his master with his luggage, and had prepared a room at Bel and the Dragon for Bev's occupancy. In obedience to his master's wishes he had taken out and pressed his evening clothes, and was now putting some cravats ready whilst Bev sat before the mirror, cleaning and paring his nails.

'Yes, I had, but something—no, some*one*— persuaded me otherwise,' he responded.

'Would I be right in thinking that the

27

someone is a lady?' asked Forbes. He had been Bev's valet for a number of years now, and was well aware of most of his master's concerns.

'You would,' agreed Bev. 'But don't assume too much. All is not as it seems.'

'As you say, sir.'

'There's no need to be so damned courteous,' answered Bev, good-humouredly. 'You won't find out any more that way. Just get out the full armoury, there's a good fellow.'

The valet looked astonished. 'The powder, sir? The patches? But I thought you said never again.'

Bev sighed. 'So I did, Forbes. So I did. But tonight I need to make an entrance that will impress, so give of your best, will you?'

* * *

As Fenella had expected, most of those attending the ball at Bel and the Dragon were familiar to them. Dudley Sampson greeted them with great pleasure, and his eyes lingered on Dora, who was looking stunning, her blue gown very flattering to her raven curls and delicately pink complexion. Mr Sampson himself looked very handsome in a plum brocade coat and breeches of a lighter shade, but although Dora greeted him kindly enough, Fenella could tell that part of her attention was on the door, for Charlie and his party had not yet arrived.

Once Dora's arrival had become generally known, several young men wandered over to pay their respects, and Fenella left the group to speak to Mrs Sandys, her old governess. Now the mother of a fine baby, Mrs Sandys was looking remarkably well, and she was delighted to meet her old pupil.

'Fenella, my dear, how pretty you look this evening. Does she not, Graham?'

'Undoubtedly, my love,' replied Mr Sandys. He too looked contented, and it seemed clear that marriage was suiting them both very well.

'Mr Sandys, you think your wife the prettiest woman in the room; deny it if you can,' said Fenella with a twinkle.

'I cannot, I confess it,' he replied, also smiling. 'But you come a very close second, Miss Parrish!'

A small commotion at the door heralded the appearance of the London party and Fenella turned to see them arrive. All the members of the party, the ladies in particular, looked very stylish and there was no mistaking London fashions. Mrs Maxfield's magenta silk gown was very low cut, showing off her magnificent bosom. Miss Maxfield, though more quietly attired, as befitted her single status, also looked very well-dressed in a cream gown with silver embroidery.

Charlie, in a snowy white wig with a sky blue coat, looked very handsome, and Fenella felt sure that Dora's heart must be skipping a beat or two at the sight of him. She had thought when he visited them that he looked exactly the same. Now, she decided, he looked a little older and more experienced. She was not entirely sure whether she liked the change. The question was, would he approach Dora, or would he confine his attentions to the members of his own party?

The band struck up with music for the first country dance and Fenella, accepting an invitation to dance from one of their near neighbours, saw Dudley approach Dora, who hesitated, glancing towards Charlie. But Charlie unhesitatingly invited Miss Maxfield to take the floor, and Dora accepted Dudley's invitation.

Charlie danced with Miss Maxfield for the first two, but when he invited Mrs Maxfield to dance with him for the next, Fenella could see the misery on Dora's face and hoped that no one else was conscious of it. She glanced around, but her acquaintance from that afternoon was nowhere to be seen. Where could he be? She sighed. Probably in the end he had felt too tired to bother; or perhaps he had had no intention of coming in the first place, and had only agreed to do so in order to keep her quiet. After all, why should he concern himself with her family's problems?

The dance had just come to a close when Fenella became conscious of a ripple of excitement passing through those gathered around the doorway. Soon afterwards, a gentleman entered the ballroom and in the manner of one very much at ease, he strolled across the now empty floor.

From his head to his heels, he was the epitome of fashion. His own hair was immaculately powdered, tied with a black ribbon, and gathered into a black silk bag. His powder and paint had been applied with unmistakable subtlety and good taste, but there was in his face a hint of danger, of which no woman in the room could possibly be unaware.

His coat was of purple satin, but the shade was of a richness that made every other purple in the room look either drab or tawdry. It fitted his broad shoulders to a nicety, and toned superbly with his silver waistcoat and pale violet small-clothes. His stockings were clocked with silver, and his measured, athletic pace demonstrated beyond all doubt that a man could walk in heeled shoes and still look like a man.

He sauntered unhesitatingly towards the London party, and just before he reached Mrs Maxfield's side, Fenella realized with astonishment that he was the same saddle-weary gentleman whom she had met that afternoon.

'My dear, who is that?' exclaimed one of two ladies standing behind Fenella.

'You mean you don't know?' replied the other. 'That's Giles Beville—Mrs Maxfield's cousin.'

'Beville! Not the Wild Marauder?'

'The very same. Watch your daughters, my dear. No woman is safe with him, so they say.'

The other woman dropped her voice, and Fenella only just heard her whisper with a low chuckle, 'Watch my daughters? My dear, such a man would be entirely wasted on them!'

It was not until Bev had almost reached his cousin's side that she turned and saw him, and having done so, she gave a cry of delight and held out her hands.

'Bev! Of all the delightful surprises!' she exclaimed. 'I thought you were still on the Continent!'

'I became conscious of a desire to speak my own language again, so I returned,' he replied, kissing her on the cheek. 'I was on my way to London, but I heard that you were staying here, and as you are my nearest relation, I decided to seek you out.'

'Should you not say "nearest and dearest"?' she suggested.

He bowed, his hand on his heart, and murmured, 'If that is your memory of the case, then who am I to argue with you?'

For a moment, the vivacious society mask disappeared, and she said cynically, 'You mean that I am your *only* relation, Bev.' She stared at him for a moment longer, then burst out laughing. 'Well, whatever might be your reason, I could not be more delighted that you have come. My dear, a provincial ball! Can you imagine? But I must say that it is exactly like you to be the last arrival at a ball, and to be so *point-device* as well! Are you preparing to break hearts tonight?'

He laughed and threw up his hands. 'By no means! But I must confess that my appearance here is not entirely accidental. I heard a rumour that one of the prettiest girls to be found hereabouts—or indeed anywhere—is to be present tonight, and you know what a weakness I have for pretty faces. I was hoping that you might be able to introduce me.'

She tapped his arm with her fan. 'Heaven help her if your fancy has lighted upon her, that's all I can say,' she said. 'If you can tell me her name I may, perhaps, oblige, but only if you promise to dance with me later.'

He bowed again. 'Her name, my dear cousin, is Miss Dora Parrish, and, of course, I am yours to command.'

'Then I will introduce you to her. But first allow me to present you to Lord Yelden, my kind host and the originator of this wonderful evening.'

A tall young man in a blue coat stepped forward, and bowed politely.

'I remember you very well, Lord Yelden,' said Bev, returning the courtesy with an elegant bow of his own. 'I trust you will forgive me for trespassing on this occasion, but when I heard that my cousin was here, I could not bear to wait a moment longer before greeting her.'

'You are very welcome, sir,' replied Charlie. 'Do you have somewhere to stay, or may I welcome you to Yelden Hall?' The words were politeness itself, but Bev seemed to sense an undercurrent of hostility. Had Charlie heard him express a desire to meet Dora? If so, it would appear that his task of arousing jealousy in the young man's breast was more than half accomplished already.

Bev shook his head. 'You are more than kind, but I have taken a room here for tonight, and as for tomorrow, I have an appointment elsewhere which I am bound to keep.'

'Another time, then,' replied Charlie.

Mrs Maxfield laid her hand on Bev's arm. 'Come along, Bev, or the fascinating Miss Parrish will be snapped up by someone else for the next dance.'

Bev turned to Charlie. 'Excuse me, my lord, but I am promised an introduction to one of the prettiest young ladies in the county.'

'Then I must not keep you,' replied Charlie unsmilingly. 'Until later, then.'

'You wicked man,' scolded Mrs Maxfield as they crossed the floor. 'That poor young man is half in love with pretty Miss Parrish himself.'

'Only half?' asked Bev with an arrested look. 'What about the rest of him?'

'Oh, I don't boast of my conquests,' replied his cousin demurely. 'But see, here she is.'

The young lady to whom his cousin was conducting him was certainly a beauty, he reflected. Her looks alone would secure her immediate success in London, whilst her manner, which appeared modest but also poised, could not be faulted. To spend a little time with such a young lady would undoubtedly be no punishment. Briefly, he thought uneasily about what his cousin had just said about her own conquests, but then there was no time to reflect any more because she was introducing him to Dora.

'Miss Parrish,' she said, as they reached Dora's side, 'the most provoking thing has occurred! Here is my cousin whom I have not seen for years, newly arrived and immediately demanding to be introduced to the prettiest woman in the room! So despite his effrontery and shocking lack of family feeling, may I present to you Mr Giles Beville? Bev, this is Miss Parrish.'

Bev bowed with a practised grace which made most other men look clumsy by comparison.

'Miss Parrish,' he murmured. 'And now, Connie, having utterly destroyed my credit, you might as well take yourself off.'

'I will,' she smiled, turning to go. 'Miss Parrish, if his continental manners should give you a disgust of him, then send him back to me.'

'It is good to discover that for once, rumour does not lie,' he murmured, after his cousin had gone.

'In what way, sir?' Dora asked him. Her voice, he was glad to note was low-pitched—although not as low as that of her sister—and pleasing.

'In saying that you are the loveliest woman in the county.'

She blushed. 'Surely not,' she replied.

'Oh, I think so. Of course,' he went on consideringly, 'I haven't quite seen them all.'

She laughed then. 'Now you are being absurd,' she told him.

'No, am I? Would you prefer me to maintain that I *had* seen them all? Now that would be an even greater absurdity. But come, I see that the next set is forming. Will you dance with me?' She glanced up at him, then at Fenella who was standing a short distance away and smiling encouragingly. Charlie was walking purposefully across the floor towards them, his face set and determined.

Suddenly remembering what her sister had said, Dora replied, 'Thank you, sir. I should like to do so.'

Charlie, who as Dora had suspected, had been on his way to ask her to dance himself, stood looking after them helplessly. Then, balked of his prey, he turned to Fenella, and putting out his hand, said imperatively, 'Come

36

on, then.'

Cherishing no illusions about his reason for asking her, Fenella curtsied, murmured, 'How could I refuse so gracious an invitation?' and put her hand in his.

He grinned reluctantly. 'I'm sorry,' he said. 'I wasn't thinking. Are you enjoying the ball? Have you danced every dance so far?'

Fenella answered his questions, but she got the distinct impression that he was not listening to a word she said and was giving all his attention to Dora and her partner.

Bev was certainly an accomplished dancer, Fenella decided. He moved gracefully, was light on his feet and his every gesture seemed to be designed to give his partner the opportunity to show off her skills to the full.

As the dance progressed, Charlie's remarks to Fenella became more and more random and his looks became blacker. No wonder, Fenella reflected, for Bev seemed to be keeping Dora very well amused, and not once did she allow her glances to stray towards Charlie. Her laughter rang out again and again, and when the dance was over, there was no doubt that she had been very well entertained. Bev led her to the side of the room, obtained a glass of champagne for her from a passing footman with a tray, and engaged her in conversation. Charlie once more took Fenella's hand and almost dragged her across the floor towards them.

'Come on,' he said again. 'Damned if that fellow is going to take her in to supper!'

They drew close to the other couple, but before Charlie could do more than open his mouth to speak, Dora said, 'Charlie, what a wonderful ball this is! I wonder, have you met Mr Beville, Mrs Maxfield's cousin?'

'Lord Yelden and I have had the pleasure of renewing our acquaintance,' murmured Bev, whilst Charlie said, 'Yes, we've met,' in tones rather less gracious.

His voice caught Dora's attention for she said to him, 'Why, Charlie, you sound quite cross. Surely Nella has not been treading on your toes? Nella, have you met Mr Beville? My sister Fenella, sir.'

'Miss Fenella,' smiled Bev, his hand on his heart. 'You put me very much in mind of someone I encountered very recently, only I cannot quite put my finger on the occasion. Could it be possible that we have met before?'

'I think not, Mr Beville,' Fenella twinkled. 'But how sad for my only distinction to lie in the fact that I remind you of somebody else!'

'Not if the someone else was entirely charming and had captivated me from the very first,' replied Bev.

During this exchange, Charlie had been trying to catch Dora's attention, and she had steadfastly refused to notice him. At first inclined to ignore her sister's suggestion that Charlie was taking her for granted, the

38

evening's events had made Dora realize that her younger sister might have had right on her side. The advent of Mr Beville and Charlie's reactions had convinced her and she resolved to teach her laggard suitor a lesson.

Dora had never enjoyed flirting. She had always thought that it was a silly pastime in which she had no skill, and she had no wish to acquire an ability which might hurt an honest man. But Bev, who was a skilled practitioner in the art, had shown her that it could be very agreeable after all. Charlie had never flirted with her; he had just assumed that she would always be there. Well, a little suspense would not hurt him.

As soon as there was a lull in the conversation between Bev and Fenella, Dora said to her sister, 'Just fancy, Mr Beville has invited me to have supper with him,' at which point there was a kind of exploding noise from Charlie, which she ignored. 'Perhaps you would like to join us—with a gentleman of your choice?'

Bev smiled to himself. In fact, he had made no such invitation. Clearly Miss Parrish was finding her feet with regard to dealing with Charlie in social settings.

'I'll come,' Charlie said swiftly.

Dora turned to him. 'I said, a gentleman of Nella's choice, not one who has imposed himself upon her,' she said calmly.

Charlie had the grace to blush. 'I beg your

pardon, Fenella,' he said. 'I was so eager to join such a . . . a merry party, that I forgot my manners. Will you please do me the honour of taking supper with me?'

Fenella, taking pity upon him because he had clearly realized how important Dora was to him after all, said, 'Thank you Charlie. That would be lovely.'

The occasion was not as lovely as it might have been, however, for although Bev and Dora chattered together in lively style, chiefly about life on the Continent, where Bev had spent so much time, Charlie put more effort into listening to their conversation than into entertaining his own partner. Luckily, Fenella was too amused by the proceedings to worry very much about any slight to herself.

After supper, Dora danced again with Bev, but after that, Charlie was waiting, and soon whisked her on to the floor. Fenella, who watched this manoeuvre with some amusement, found her laughter being returned by a smiling Bev. Having seen how graceful he was, she was rather hoping that he might dance with her next, but a moment later, she saw his cousin approach him, and soon afterwards he led her on to the floor.

She consoled herself with the thought that there was still time for him to dance with her later, but no sooner had the music ended, than her father approached her.

'Nella, my dear, your mama feels one of her

heads coming on. I think that it would be best if we were to leave now.'

Swallowing her disappointment at the sudden curtailment of the evening, she said, 'Of course, Papa. You look after Mama, and I'll go and get Dora.'

Charlie and Dora came off the floor looking as though they had been quarrelling, and when Fenella explained the situation, Charlie looked disappointed.

'I'll call and see you tomorrow,' he said meaningfully to Dora.

Fenella expected her gentle sister to blush and say how pleased she would be, but to her surprise, she tossed her head and said, 'Bring all your friends with you if you like.'

'I'll come alone,' he answered deliberately.

'Suit yourself, sir,' she replied, in the same tone as before.

They were all silent in the carriage going home, out of consideration for Lady Parrish's headache, but after they had arrived and Mama had been settled in her room with some warm milk, Fenella went to Dora's room and scratched on the door.

'Dora, that did the trick,' she said. 'I'll wager anything you like that Charlie will propose when he comes here tomorrow.'

'I don't know whether I shall receive him or not,' answered the new, confident Dora of the ballroom. Then a moment later, she looked shyly at her sister and said, 'Oh Nella, do you think he will?'

'Of course,' replied her sister embracing her. Then after a few moments, she said casually, 'How fortunate that Mr Beville came and decided to flirt with you this evening.'

'Yes it was, wasn't it? I did hear that his reputation is very bad, but such things are not always deserved. As you know, I have never enjoyed flirting at all before, but Nella, it really was very pleasant. Do you suppose that was just because he is very good at it?'

Fenella agreed that this might be so, and was conscious of a moment's regret that she had had no opportunity to experience Bev's flirting technique at first hand. She toyed with the idea of saying that she had asked him to flirt with Dora, but then decided against it. Her older sister was very tolerant of her ways, but she just might take exception to Fenella's introducing herself to a complete stranger who turned out to be the Wild Marauder.

*   *   *

It was customary on the day following a ball for a gentleman to visit any lady with whom he had danced the previous evening. It occurred to Fenella that Bev might come and visit her sister for that reason. The same thought had also occurred to Charlie, however, and he was therefore at Brightstones asking to see Sir Humphrey before the ladies were even

42

dressed.

Fenella was the nearest to being ready, for she was always an early riser, but once it was known that Lord Yelden had come and was with the master, every hand, including Fenella's, was pressed into service in order to get Dora ready as quickly as possible.

The interview with Sir Humphrey was soon concluded, and Dora was only just ready when the message came to ask Miss Parrish 'please to step down to the master's study.'

Despite her bold words of the previous night, Dora hurried downstairs, her eyes shining, and Fenella and her mother followed at a more measured pace, to await events in the blue saloon. They tried to make conversation, but even with the previous night's ball (which would normally have been a fruitful topic) to discuss, it was hard to think of anything other than the interview which was taking place. Whilst Lady Parrish paced about restlessly, Fenella wandered over to the window and stood looking out. Part of the folly could just be seen from the windows.

After what seemed like a lifetime, but was in reality only about ten minutes, Dora came in, her face aglow, followed by her father and Charlie. Then there was nothing but hugs and kisses and congratulations. Charlie was urged to dine with them that evening, and this he agreed to do.

'My friends will excuse me, I know, when

they hear my tidings,' he said with a smile.

After he had gone, Sir Humphrey disappeared into his study, and Lady Parrish and Dora seemed to be anxious to talk about dates and weddings, so Fenella took the opportunity of slipping out of the house to go and sit on her wall. She could not explain it, but she had a feeling that Bev might come riding by. She told herself that she just wanted to thank him and to tell him about the happy result of their plans, but if she was honest with herself, she had to admit that she wanted to see him again.

She did not have long to wait before she heard the sound of a horse making a leisurely progress on the other side of the perimeter wall, and soon Giles Beville came into view. He smiled when he saw her.

'May I come in?' he asked her. She nodded and while he came in through the gate, she scrambled down off her perch. By mutual unspoken agreement, they wandered over to the same piece of wall on which they had sat on the previous occasion. 'I can hardly bear to ask,' he said, as soon as they were settled. 'Were your machinations successful?'

'*Our* machinations,' she corrected him. 'You were in the plot as much as I.' He raised his brows quizzically and she had the grace to blush. 'Well, perhaps not quite as much,' she conceded. She studied him critically. He looked very different in the daylight, without his paint and powder and that gorgeous purple satin. He was dressed in very much the same way as he had been when she had first met him the previous day, but he had lost the tired, almost dispirited look that he had worn on that occasion.

'You still haven't told me whether your— our—plans met with success,' he reminded her.

'Yes they did—with excellent success,' she replied. 'Charlie arrived almost in time for breakfast, and has asked for Dora's hand. As I left the house, Mama and Dora were starting to talk of wedding dresses.'

'I should have thought that you would have wanted to play a part in that discussion.'

'Yes, well, I suppose one's own wedding dress must be very fascinating, but I can't get excited about someone else's, even Dora's just yet, I'm afraid.' She fell silent.

'Forgive my saying so, but you sound slightly less enchanted than I had expected,' ventured Bev.

'You're very perceptive,' she told him. 'I have always been very sure that Charlie was the right man for Dora. In fact, I had no doubt that he was, and I still think I'm right, it's just that . . .' She was silent again.

'Just that what?' he prompted.

'Oh, I just wish he could have come straight to Dora's side, without having been made to feel jealous by the attentions paid to her by

45

another man.'

He laughed lightly. 'My clear, you mustn't judge him too harshly,' he said. 'We men are contrary creatures, prone to despise what we have, and longing for what is beyond our grasp. It's a sad fact, but true.'

'I think that's horrible,' said Fenella, wrinkling her brow. 'And if it really is true, I don't think I want to marry at all.'

'Why on earth not?'

'Well it means that we are for ever being judged by what's on the surface.'

'Perhaps that is because, in the case of some of your sex, that is all there is.'

She stared at him. 'Someone must have hurt you dreadfully, to make you feel like that,' she whispered.

He stared at her unblinkingly for a moment before laughing out loud. 'What an intriguing notion,' he said lightly. 'But never fear, my dear. Some man of intelligence will manage to look beyond your very prepossessing exterior and value the intriguing character that lies behind it.'

'You think I'm intriguing?' she ventured tentatively.

'Oh undoubtedly,' he laughed.

'Why are you laughing at me now?' she asked him suspiciously.

'It's simply that you immediately responded to my compliment to your character, and ignored what I said about your appearance.'

He stood up. 'As soon as I think I have the measure of your sex, one of you manages to astound me yet again. But that simply proves what I have always suspected.'

'And what is that?' asked Fenella, also standing up.

'Why, that your sex is by far the superior,' he replied lightly.' And now, I must go. Pray give my excuses to Miss Parrish, if you think it appropriate. Under the present circumstances, I don't feel that I will be anything other than *de trop* in your house today—especially in view of my determined pursuit of your sister last night.'

'No, I suppose not,' she said regretfully. 'Is it really true that you are called the Wild Marauder?'

'Now, where did you hear that?' he asked her as they walked over to his horse.

'I overheard two ladies talking last night,' she admitted. '*Is* it true?'

'Yes, I'm afraid it is,' he admitted, taking hold of his horse's bridle. 'But in my defence, I must say that it's a title I acquired some years ago, and have been trying to live down ever since.'

'Well, I don't think you're at all wild,' said Fenella. 'I think you're very kind.'

He took hold of her chin and, bending, kissed her gently on the mouth.

'My dear child, you don't know the half of it,' he said, before mounting his horse. He inclined his head politely, put his hat on his head, and rode out of the gate and down the road.

After he had gone, Fenella touched her lips tentatively with her fingers. It was the first kiss that she had ever received from someone outside her own family, and it had been from the Wild Marauder. That would surely be something to boast about—except that she could never tell anyone!

CHAPTER FOUR

It was generally agreed that when Miss Dora Parrish was married in Cookham Parish Church, she was the loveliest bride that had been seen there for many a long day. As if to confirm this view, the weather, which had been overcast for several days previously, much to the anxiety of Lady Parrish, cleared up and the bride arrived at the church in brilliant sunshine.

Dora and Fenella and their mother had paid a special visit to London in order to purchase material for the gown, and the gasps from the waiting villagers when Dora emerged from the carriage in a gown of white satin embroidered with silver confirmed that the trip had been worth while. That had not been the only purchase that had been made, however, for a length of lilac satin had been purchased for Fenella, who was to be her sister's only bridesmaid. As she viewed herself in the pier glass in her bedroom just before it was time for her to join the others downstairs, she decided that she had never looked so well. Dark-brown waves could not compete with black curls, nor could twinkling hazel eyes against dreamy blue ones, but she knew that she looked becoming, and perhaps some gentleman might agree with her. After all, Dora was now spoken for!

All at once, she found herself thinking about Mr Beville. A few days ago, she had discovered that he was to attend the wedding. This had surprised her at first, for she knew that since he had only just returned from the Continent, neither Dora nor Charlie knew him very well. Furthermore, Charlie had been glaring at Bev like a dog who thought that its bone was in danger of being snatched up by another. She could only conclude that the engagement, together with the relationship that already existed between Charlie and the Maxfields, had smoothed the way between the two men.

She wondered how Mr Beville would be dressed for the wedding. Would he be in powder and paint, as on the night of the ball, or would he look more like the country gentleman whom she had first met when she had been perched on the wall of the folly? She had surreptitiously looked out for him when they had paid that brief shopping visit to London, but, perhaps not surprisingly, without success. Whatever he might be wearing, she could not deny that she was looking forward to seeing him again. He was so utterly unlike anyone she had ever met before.

The wedding was generally agreed to be a delightful occasion. Charlie, dressed in snowy white waistcoat and breeches and a blue coat, looked handsome and eager; and Mr Maxfield, who acted as Charlie's groomsman, played his part with grace.

After the register had been signed, the happy couple left the church, Dora looking so radiant that Fenella felt that her efforts had all been worthwhile. Mr Maxfield offered her his arm as they walked down the aisle after the newly married pair.

'Happy ever after,' he commented.

'Yes,' she replied with a deep sigh.

It was at that moment that she caught sight of Bev in a coat of burgundy brocade. Her deep delight at this happy conclusion could still be seen in the expression on her face, and consequently as she turned to look at him the sweetness of her smile almost took his breath away.

After the wedding, they returned to Brightstones for the wedding breakfast. As well as Bev, some of Charlie's other friends had come from London, and Fenella recognized Mrs Maxfield and her husband and sister-in-law.

The bride and groom were only to go to Yelden Hall that night after which they were to spend a little time at the house of a friend of Charlie's in Hertfordshire, before taking up residence in London.

'How will you like living away from the country?' Fenella had asked her, for Dora had always been a country girl.

'I expect I shall like it very well,' Dora had replied placidly. 'After all, Charlie and I will be together, and that is the most important thing. And in any case, we can always come back to Yelden Hall, you know.'

There was quite a crowd gathered at Brightstones for the wedding breakfast, and everyone appeared to be enjoying themselves. Everyone except, perhaps, for Dudley Sampson, Fenella noted. When he knew that anyone's eye was upon him, he smiled brightly and talked cheerfully. But when he believed that he was unobserved, the smile disappeared and instead, he looked moodily down into his glass. From what Fenella could see, he appeared to be replenishing it rather frequently.

She was fond of Dudley and his sister Augusta. Although their family had not lived in the vicinity for as long as the Parrishes—for the house where Dudley and Augusta lived had been built by their grandfather, whereas the Parrishes had been in the vicinity for six generations—the present generation of young people had grown up almost as brothers and sisters.

Dudley had been in love with Dora for almost as long as Fenella could remember, but although Dora regarded him with affection, it was Charlie who had always had her heart. Dudley must have known that he did not have a chance with her, but nevertheless the reality of the wedding had clearly hit him hard.

As Fenella stood observing him, someone leaned over to speak to him and abruptly he stood up, knocking his glass over, and disappeared on to the terrace. After only a very brief hesitation, she followed him and Bev, who until now had been detained by his cousin, and who had been about to approach Fenella, watched her go.

It did not take her very long to find Dudley. As she had supposed, he had gone to a small enclosed garden with stone benches around the sides and a rose garden in the centre. It had always been a popular place for the young people to gather.

He sat with his elbows resting on his knees, his face in his hands, but at the sound of her gown rustling, he looked up, his unguarded expression wearing a look of hope until he realized who it was.

'Dudley, I'm so sorry,' she said, sitting down next to him, 'but it was always going to be this way, you know.'

'Yes, I know,' he answered wretchedly. 'I never really had any hope; not really. But when Charlie stayed in London for such a long time, I began to wonder if . . .' He broke off, shaking his head. 'I shouldn't be burdening you with my sorrows. This should be a happy day for you.'

Fenella laid a hand on his arm but did not say anything. She was convinced that Charlie and Dora were made for each other, but she could not help recalling how she had had to enlist Bev's aid in order to remind Charlie of Dora's attractions. Much though she told herself that Charlie would have come to his senses later if not sooner, a tiny part of her brain whispered that if Charlie had not claimed Dora at the ball, then perhaps Dudley would have had a chance.

'Dudley, I'm so sorry,' she said again, after a long silence. 'I wish I could do something to help.'

He looked at her and smiled. 'You're a good friend,' he said, 'and a lovely girl. Why couldn't I have had the sense to fall in love with you instead?'

He leaned towards her and kissed her on her cheek, then, after a moment's hesitation, he gently turned her face towards him and kissed her more lingeringly on her mouth. Quite what would have happened next it is impossible to say, for there was a sound of a throat being cleared, and at once they sprang apart.

'Pardon me if I intrude,' said a familiar voice, 'but the bride and groom are about to leave.' It was Bev, his single raised eyebrow giving him an ironic expression.

'I must come at once, then,' said Fenella, getting to her feet and shaking out her skirts. She was hoping that she was not blushing too much.

'I think I will remain here, if you do not think that I will be missed,' said Dudley. 'Fenella . . .' She turned back to face him and, as she did so, he took hold of her hand and kissed it. 'Thank you.' She smiled and left the garden, with Bev politely ushering her ahead of him.

She hurried on, hoping to avoid discussing the scene that had just taken place, but he hurried after her and caught hold of her arm.

'One moment,' he said.

She stopped and he let go of her at once. 'I do not want to miss my sister,' she said.

'Ah,' he murmured, straightening his cuffs. 'I'm afraid I was not exactly truthful just then.'

'Then why did you say what you did?' she asked him. 'And why did you follow me? You did follow me, didn't you?'

'Yes I did,' he replied imperturbably, 'and I did so precisely in order to prevent the kind of indiscretion which I have just witnessed.'

'I was not being indiscreet,' she retorted. 'I

54

have known Dudley all my life.'

'I've no doubt that you have,' he replied. 'But how many of the guests present today know that?'

'I don't care what they know,' she answered him defiantly.

'Then it clearly behoves others to care on your behalf. Or are you looking for an excuse to become engaged to him?'

'Pooh!' she answered him rudely. 'It would never have come to that.'

'It certainly might have done had it been my cousin who discovered you,' he replied. 'Everything she sees is around London by the following day.'

'But we are not in London,' she declared positively. Then she stopped speaking abruptly.

'Precisely,' he said. 'We may not be in London, but we are surrounded by those who go there, are we not? Soon your sister will be living there. When does she expect to bring you out? Next year? Will she want to do it if your reputation is damaged already?'

She stared at him for a few minutes in silence, then said, 'Why are you so concerned about my reputation, anyway? I would have thought that you of all people would not have cared two straws about such things.'

His eyes narrowed. 'You mean because I am called the Wild Marauder, I suppose? It's precisely because I *am* so experienced with regard to reputations and the loss of them that I can presume to advise you now.'

'Well you presume too far,' she declared. 'Now if you have finished droning on I shall go and find my sister!' She turned to go back to the house, but he caught hold of her arm again, and this time he did not release her.

'Droning on, you say?' he drawled. 'Perhaps you would take more notice of my warning if I gave you a practical demonstration of why you should avoid being alone with men in such secluded spots!' So saying, he pulled her firmly against him and bent to kiss her hard on her mouth.

When at last he drew his head back, she tore herself free and ran towards the house, her face flaming, her skirts flying behind her. He stood staring after her for a few moments before following her into the house.

CHAPTER FIVE

It occurred to Fenella as she wandered down into the village of Cookham, that she had never thought how much she would miss the company of her sister. It had always been an accepted thing, ever since they were old enough to think about the matter, that Dora would marry Charlie. Of course Fenella realized that that would mean that Dora would no longer be living at Brightstones. She had always supposed, however, that Charlie and Dora would settle at Yelden Hall, only a short ride away, and that she would be able to visit her sister all the time. Indeed, Dora had said as much at the wedding breakfast six months ago.

'We'll soon be together again, you'll see,' Dora had told Fenella, just before she and Charlie drove away together in his barouche, pulled by a matched pair of bay horses. 'We'll see each other every day, just as we've always planned.' But this had not come about, at least not yet, and it was hard for Fenella not to feel lonely and even a little disappointed.

Dora and Charlie were now living in London, and all the letters that Fenella had received from her sister seemed to indicate that she was enjoying London life. But Fenella could not believe that her sister would never want to come to the country. Three months ago, they had received the glad tidings that Dora was expecting a child, and they had all been sure that Dora would want to come home and have her baby at Yelden Hall, where Charlie himself had been born, and his father before him. But Charlie had insisted that she must remain in London, close to the best physicians. Whilst regretting this decision for their own sakes, Sir Humphrey and Lady Parrish and Fenella were all pleased that Charlie was so concerned for the well-being of his wife and child.

Christmas would have been very dismal had it not been for the arrival of the Grindles in the neighbourhood. Mr Grindle, it was understood, was a wealthy merchant anxious to establish himself outside London. Mr and Mrs Grindle were looking for a property to rent or even to buy, and they had taken a fancy to the area around Cookham. They seemed pleasant people, and very genteel, and their son Simon, who had attended school with Dudley Sampson, was a lively young man with an impish sense of humour, and he had cheered up many an occasion over the Christmas season.

One bit of excitement that they could very well have done without had been that just after Christmas, Sir Humphrey had taken a heavy fall from his horse and broken his leg in three places. He was proving to be a very bad patient, taxing to his valet, his wife, his daughter and everyone in the house. The most patient member of the family with the sick and fractious had always been Dora, but, of course, Dora was no longer there.

Fenella sighed as she entered Cookham and began to walk along the main street. The last time that she had walked to the village with Dora had been the day before the wedding.

'Let's go together, one last time,' Dora had said, taking her sister's arm and squeezing it. It had been a warm, sunny day on that occasion, and the two young women had only needed light shawls. They had dawdled together, stopping to talk to well-wishers and lingering to look in the window of the haberdasher's. Today, on a cold morning in February, Fenella pulled her cloak more closely around her, and walked purposefully to the shop. There would be no strolling or lingering in this chilly wind!

As she came out of the shop, her purchase made, her eye was caught by a length of material on display. It was almost the same shade as the gown that she had worn for Dora's wedding. Suddenly, she thought of Bev, and of how he had kissed her the last time they had met. They had not spoken to one another after the incident and Fenella had wondered whether he had regretted his actions, for fear that the naive country girl might read more into them than he had intended. He need not have worried, she told herself for the hundredth time. His kiss meant nothing to her, but because of the service he had rendered her, she did wish that their acquaintance might have ended in a more cordial way.

Her mood of introspection was interrupted when she heard herself spoken to, and turning, she saw Dudley Sampson, his hat in his hand. He really was exceptionally handsome, Fenella reflected, the weak February sun bringing out the gold in his hair, but she decided that he was looking older. Clearly, Dora's marriage had hit him hard.

'A cold day, is it not?' he said, smiling.

'Very cold,' she replied.

The day after the wedding he had come to Brightstones and having gained a private interview with her, he had apologized handsomely for his behaviour in the gardens.

'I fear I drank too much, and indeed am paying for it today,' he had said ruefully. 'I am very ashamed at having embarrassed you by my unseemly conduct.'

Fenella had assured him sincerely that she quite understood, but she had ventured to ask him whether he had spoken to Mr Beville about the matter. He had shaken his head and told her that Mr Beville had left soon after the departure of the newly married couple. It was impossible to tell what Bev had thought concerning the scene that he had witnessed; and it irked her that she had never had a chance to explain to him how matters really stood between herself and Dudley.

After the conventional greetings, Dudley said, 'I wonder, would you care to come to the Dovecote with me—that is, if you haven't any more pressing matters to attend to? Augusta will be pleased to see you, and I . . . that is to say, there is a matter which is troubling me considerably, and . . .' His voice faded away. Fenella looked at his face again and could see that he did indeed look anxious.

'By all means,' she replied readily. 'My shopping is done and I should be delighted to see Augusta. I'll certainly help you if I can, or at any rate listen.'

A look of relief crossed his face and he offered her his arm, but under his breath, he murmured, 'I fear that this is beyond mending.'

The Dovecote was a charming house, just on the outskirts of Cookham on the Maidenhead road. It was a neat white house, very well kept, and earned its name because of the existence of a very old dovecote in the grounds at the back. This construction was considerably older than the house itself and had probably been established by a small group of monks who had settled there in years gone by. All other traces of the monks had vanished, but the dovecote remained, and Dudley's grandfather, wisely resisting the impulse to demolish such an ancient building, had built his own house in front of it and named it after that venerable structure.

Dudley's sister was setting tiny stitches into some exquisite embroidery, and she got up to greet Fenella warmly. She was a pretty woman with her brother's open countenance but with hair of a lighter shade, and she was a little older than Dora. She had been married briefly to a captain of dragoons, but after his death in action three years ago, she had returned to her family home to be housekeeper and companion for her brother.

After her exposure to the raw February

wind, the roaring fire burning in the grate was very welcome, and Fenella walked over to it to warm her hands.

'It is very cold out, is it not?' said Augusta, after she had rung for tea. 'I think perhaps it is the coldest day that we have had this year.'

Fenella agreed. 'As I walked into the village today, I was thinking about how Dora and I had strolled there on the day before the wedding in just our shawls.'

'You were glad of your cloak today, I'm sure,' replied Augusta. 'Is Dora well?'

The conversation continued in this pleasant, undemanding fashion until after the butler had brought the tea. As soon as he had left the room, Augusta said carefully, 'Has Dora said anything about her plans for where the baby is to be born?'

Fenella shook her head. 'She has said nothing in her letters,' she replied. 'I know that she always intended to be confined at Yelden Hall, but Charlie has declared that she must remain in London to be near the doctor, for safety's sake. No doubt they will all come to Yelden Hall when the baby is safely born.' She noticed a look pass between Dudley and Augusta, and she said in a more anxious tone, 'What is it? You know something, don't you?'

Dudley looked again at his sister and said, 'I suppose, strictly speaking, I should not say anything, but I cannot reconcile it with my conscience to keep silent.' Fenella looked at him expectantly. 'You may know that I am a little acquainted with Mr Grindle. That is to say, I knew him a little before he came to live here. In fact his son was at school with me, only a couple of years beneath me, and Mr Grindle was kind enough to take an interest in me.'

'What Dudley means, Fenella, is that some of the boys would have bullied Simon Grindle because he was a merchant's son, but Dudley admitted him to his circle of friends and so was able to protect him.'

'That was well done,' said Fenella approvingly. Dudley coloured. An unassuming man, he hated to hear himself praised.

'Augusta makes too much of it,' he said. 'But to continue, as I expect you know, Mr and Mrs Grindle have been staying with friends in Maidenhead whilst they have been looking around to find a property to rent. They came here to drink tea with us a few days ago, and Mr Grindle revealed that he had a matter that he wanted to discuss with me.' He paused for a moment, then he said, looking anxiously at Fenella, 'He has had a letter from Charlie, offering to let Yelden Hall to him.'

Fenella stared at him, her expression absolutely aghast. 'Charlie is prepared to let the Hall? I don't believe it!' she exclaimed. 'I know for a fact that Dora is counting on coming to the Hall when the baby is born! Are you sure that you are not mistaken?'

Dudley nodded slowly and reluctantly. 'He did not show me the letter,' he said, 'but he told me that Charlie was quite definite about the matter. He wants to let the Hall. Mr Grindle likes the place very much, and wants to accept Charlie's suggestion, but he does not know how well it will be received locally.'

'As to that, the Grindles seem to be well liked,' responded Fenella. 'I don't think they will meet with any opposition. But I still don't understand it,' she went on, in tones of consternation. 'Why let the Hall, just when he is newly married and surely needs a home to which he can bring his bride?' She was silent for a moment, then said, 'I wonder if Dora knows? Certainly she has not even given so much as a hint of such a thing in her letters.'

'Would she want to say anything about it?' Augusta asked tentatively. 'Would she not want to remain silent—out of loyalty to Charlie?'

'I suppose so,' agreed Fenella doubtfully. 'But whatever will Papa say?'

'You must not say anything to him,' said Dudley quickly. 'Mr Grindle told me this in confidence, but did give permission for me to tell Augusta. I am not at all easy in my conscience about having told you this now, but I would have felt equally guilty had I remained silent. It might be that when Dora learns the news you will have the chance to support her in some way.'

'Yes, perhaps. Thank you for telling me.' She paused for a few moments, then said, 'Are you planning to go to London yourselves for any of the season this year?' After a little stilted conversation which captured the interest of no one present, Fenella left, promising to come again soon.

As she walked back home, her attention was entirely given to the extraordinary tidings that she had just heard. Ever since Charlie had had the chance of choosing his own place of residence, he had demonstrated a definite preference for the town over the country. Fenella had never supposed for one minute, however, that he would actually consider letting the Hall.

If Dora had agreed to this decision, then she must have changed a great deal, Fenella decided. She had always loved the country, only ever going to London under sufferance, and furthermore she had spoken about how she would enjoy redesigning the garden of Yelden Hall after she and Charlie were married. Such comments would not normally be made by someone who knew that the house would soon be let to another. If only she could go to Dora and find out what was really going on, she thought to herself. Such a sensitive subject could not be explored through correspondence.

She was not at all sure how she would be able to conceal what she had heard from her parents, but no sooner had she entered the house, than her mother hurried out into the hall, a letter in her hand.

'My dear, such news!' she exclaimed. 'Come into the drawing-room while I tell you!'

Fenella handed her outdoor things to Berry, and followed her mother into the cosy drawing-room. It was by no means the grandest room at Brightstones, but it was by far the warmest in winter, and the family usually sat there unless there was a large number of visitors to be entertained.

'What is your news, Mama?' Fenella asked her, pleased to be given a distraction from the unwelcome thoughts which had been absorbing her all the way back from Cookham.

'A letter from Dora,' replied her mother. 'She was so sorry not to be able to come home for Christmas, but Charlie will not hear of her travelling whilst she is increasing. But her pregnancy is making her a little dispirited, and she thinks that the very thing to cheer her up would be to have you to stay. You are to have a season in London, my love, just as we have always planned!'

CHAPTER SIX

As Fenella travelled the mere thirty-five miles which separated Cookham from London, she wondered, not for the first time, whether her sister's low spirits were to be attributed solely to her condition. She had said nothing to her parents about what Dudley and Augusta had disclosed. This had not been entirely easy, for Mama had been speculating about how long it would be before Dora would bring the baby back to Yelden Hall, so that the new Viscount Burchett—if indeed it was a boy—and his mama could benefit from some country air.

It had not been easy either to leave Mama behind to deal with Papa on her own. His leg was mending well, but he was still not allowed out and he had reached the stage when everything appeared to annoy him, and he saved his worst moods for those who loved him best. Lady Parrish had insisted, however.

'To be honest with you, I have been hoping that Dora would invite you to London and introduce you into society,' she said. 'It will be such an opportunity for you. And do not worry about Papa. In some ways, I shall manage him much better if I only have him to think about.'

During the early days of Sir Humphrey's convalescence, it had been the young men of the neighbourhood who had come to his rescue. Both Dudley and Simon had been to Brightstones to play chess or draughts with him, and their company had helped him to while away the weary hours. Sometimes, Augusta had accompanied her brother, and then they had all made a merry party.

Fenella smiled to herself as she leaned back against the squabs of her father's well-sprung chaise, and recollected some of the amusing things that Simon had said. It had been good to see Augusta laugh again. She had become rather serious since the death of her captain of dragoons, and Fenella wondered whether she and Simon would make a match of it. She knew that Lady Parrish had had half an eye on the lively merchant's son for her younger daughter, but she herself was not at all smitten. For one thing, Simon did not seem to regard her in a romantic way; for another, a more darkly saturnine figure tended to haunt her dreams. Would she see Bev in London, she wondered? Or would he merely think of her as a young girl whom he had rescued from indiscretion but whom he was now anxious to avoid?

She was roused from her reverie by the slowing down of the chaise, and Millie her maid, nodding opposite her, woke up. When they had come to a halt, Robert, the groom, sprang down and came to the window.

'One of the horses has cast a shoe, Miss Fenella,' he said. 'We're only a mile or so short of Hounslow, but we'll have to go at a walk till we get there.'

'All right, Robert,' replied Fenella with a sigh. 'It appears we have no choice. Will we still be able to get to London tonight?'

'Oh yes, miss, unless all the blacksmiths in

Hounslow have died and gone to Heaven,' he replied, with somewhat lugubrious humour. 'We'll go to the Swan and you can have a comfortable place to sit and get something to drink maybe while we get Russet seen to.'

Up until now, Fenella had been so lost in cogitation that she had been unaware of the passage of time. Now that the train of her thought had been broken, however, their progress seemed to be unbearably slow, and she was almost screaming with frustration by the time they arrived at the Swan. Her annoyance was not lessened by the fact that the slightest degree of motion seemed to be sufficient to send Millie into a deep sleep, and consequently she was of no use as company at all.

'Come on, Millie, for goodness' sake,' said Fenella, more impatiently than she had intended. The maid woke up good-humouredly enough, and the two of them got down with Robert's assistance.

'I'll bespeak a private parlour for you, Miss Fenella,' said the groom, then turning to Millie, he added, 'Have a care to your mistress, now. This is a public inn, remember.' So saying, he went on ahead of them with Millie grumbling as they followed on.

'As if I didn't know this was a public inn. I can use my eyes, can't I? As if I wouldn't look after you . . .' She continued in much the same vein as they entered the Swan, and Fenella, her attention wandering, looked around to see a group of very fashionably dressed people emerging from one of the rooms, obviously preparing to leave. There were four women and three men. The women went past, in a cloud of frills, perfume and chatter, and were followed soon after by the men who had paused in order to pay the landlord.

'Are you coming with us, Bev?' one of the women asked over her shoulder, as the men drew level with Fenella, and one of them stood back to allow her to pass. She looked up quickly—for she had been trying hard not to stare at strangers, as her mother had taught her—and realized that he was Giles Beville. He was dressed for riding, much as he had been when she had last seen him, but she now realized, seeing him with this fashionable group, how well he fitted in with them. There was about his comparatively simple garb an unmistakable air of style.

She was preparing to greet him, but, as he walked past, his eyes slid over her without a spark of recognition, and he walked on as if he had never met her before, calling out to the woman who had spoken to him, 'Where else should I go, my sweet?'

Surprised and a little hurt, she turned to glance after him, but before she could do or say anything, the landlord approached her, saying, 'I understand from your man, ma'am, that you've had a bit of a mishap on the road.

70

If you'll follow me, I've a private parlour with a good fire burning, where you can have some refreshment until your horse has been shod.'

Fenella and Millie followed him into the parlour where, true to his word, the fire was burning merrily. He stooped to put some more coal on it and, as he did so, went on apologetically, 'I'm sorry about those females, miss. The gentlemen are good customers of mine, but they've never brought such to my inn before, and I hope will not do so again, for this is a respectable place. Was it tea you'll be wanting, miss?'

'Yes, if you please,' replied Fenella, drawing off her gloves. She thought back to the appearance of the four women, and now recalled that they had perhaps been dressed rather more flamboyantly than was either necessary or appropriate for travelling. Who were they, she wondered? Especially, who was the woman whom Bev had addressed as 'my sweet'?

'Look, Miss Fenella, here's the tea,' said Millie a few minutes later. They sat down to drink it, and it was not very long after they had finished that news came that Russet had now been given a new shoe, and that it was time for them to set out once more.

Fenella's visits to London had been rare and few, and despite the fact that she had been very recently with Dora and Mama in order to buy material for their wedding finery, she still

71

found herself very interested in all that was going on as they passed through the streets. Millie slept on, and Fenella was torn between wanting to rouse the girl so that she could take in the scene, and leaving her to sleep so that she could enjoy it by herself in peace. In the end, she took the more selfish decision, but lost any feeling of guilt that she might have had when they got down outside Charlie and Dora's house in Curzon Street and Millie said, 'Oh, that was a lovely sleep. I feel as fresh as a daisy now, miss.'

After the news that she had had from Dudley, Fenella was a little uncertain as to what she might find, but she was reassured when a radiant Dora flew into her arms, crying, 'Nella! Dearest Nella! Oh, how happy I am to see you! For how long can Mama spare you? A good long time, I hope.'

Fenella laughed. 'I'm glad to hear you say so, for I think that Mama is hoping that you will introduce me into society,' she replied.

'Of course I shall,' replied Dora smiling. 'Millie, are you well? Did you enjoy the journey?'

'Yes thank you, Miss Dora—Lady Yelden, I should say,' replied Millie, dropping a curtsy.

'Measures will make sure that you are well settled,' replied Dora. 'But you need not worry about my sister, Measures. I will show her to her room myself.'

'Very good, my lady,' replied the butler with

72

a bow.

'Why are you giggling, Nella?' Dora asked her sister as she took hold of her by the hand.

'It's just Millie,' replied Fenella. 'How she can say that she enjoyed the journey I do not know, for she slept through every bit of it, from start to finish!'

'How is Papa?' Dora asked.

'Cross and grumpy. I felt rather guilty at leaving Mama to manage him by herself, really.'

'I expect she'll manage him much better when she's on her own with him,' said Dora wisely.

'Yes, that's what she said,' Fenella agreed. She looked around her. 'This is a lovely house, Dora.'

'Yes, it is, isn't it?' agreed Dora. 'It's rented, you know.'

Fenella halted on the stairs. 'Doesn't Charlie own a house in London, then?' she asked her sister.

'Come on,' said Dora impatiently, pulling at Fenella's hand. 'No, he doesn't. There was a Yelden House in Grosvenor Square, but Charlie's grandfather sold it, and it was pulled down and something else was built there instead. But I think that it's much more convenient to rent a house. Lots of people do, you know; and after all, we always have Yelden Hall.'

Fortunately by this time, they had reached

the door to Fenella's bedchamber and in exclaiming truthfully about what a charming room it was, Fenella was excused from making any response to what Dora had just said.

'Do you want me to go away while you tidy yourself, or shall I stay so that we can talk?' Dora asked, so obviously favouring the second alternative.

'Oh, don't go away,' answered Fenella. 'You wouldn't have done if we were still at home, would you?' Dora stared at her for a moment, and Fenella, looking at her own reflection in the mirror, saw that behind her, her sister's eyes were filling with tears. She turned around and hurried to Dora's side, putting her arms around her. 'Dora! Whatever can be the matter?' she said.

Dora wiped away her tears. 'Nothing really,' she replied, trying to smile. 'It's just that when you said the word *home* it reminded me how much I would have liked to have my baby at Yelden Hall. But Charlie says that he wants me to be in town so that if need be, he can call in the very best of doctors. But it won't be necessary, Nella, I know that. I feel so very well, and I know that I should feel even better in the country. But Charlie won't hear of it.'

Fenella waited for her sister to say something about the fact that Yelden Hall was to be let to the Grindles, but she did not do so. Surely Charlie could not be thinking of letting the house without telling his wife? She opened her mouth to say something, but closed it again. The last thing that she wanted to do was to cause trouble between husband and wife; but she resolved to speak to Charlie at the earliest opportunity. If he had not said anything to Dora about letting the house, he must be persuaded to do so, before she discovered about it from some other source.

There was not to be an opportunity of doing so that evening. Charlie did indeed come back to the house shortly after Fenella had arrived, whilst the ladies were enjoying a cup of tea, and he greeted his sister-in-law with every evidence of affection.

'I do declare you've grown, Nella,' he said, holding her at arm's length with both hands, after he had given her a brotherly kiss. 'Don't you think she's taller, Dora?'

'Perhaps a little,' agreed his wife, smiling at him adoringly. 'But we shall soon see when we go clothes' shopping tomorrow.'

Charlie groaned and struck his forehead. 'I regret to say, then, that I shall be forced to find a prior engagement,' he declared. 'There's nothing I dislike more.'

'We shan't need you, anyway,' replied Dora. 'In fact, we shall do better on our own, shan't we, Nella? But we must make plans for what we're going to do whilst Nella's with us, Charlie, and I thought that we could start doing that this evening over dinner.'

He smiled. 'That sounds an excellent

notion, my love, but I pray that you will hold me excused for tonight. I have another engagement, I'm afraid.'

Dora looked disappointed. 'Oh Charlie no, surely not on Nella's first night here?'

'I'm afraid so,' he repeated.

'But Charlie, you have known for several days that Nella was coming today, and . . .'

Seeing that Charlie was starting to look harassed, Fenella said quickly, 'It's all right, Dora. I haven't seen you for ages, and am longing for a comfortable prose. We shall do much better without any gentlemen, you know.'

Charlie's brow cleared. 'That's the ticket,' he said cheerfully. 'You can abuse me much better without my being present, I'm sure. I'd better go and change my dress, or I shall never be ready.' He went to the door.

'Where are you going, Charlie?' Dora asked him. Her tone was cheerful, but there was an edge to her voice which might have denoted anxiety.

'Oh, I'm just meeting a few fellows at my club,' he said carelessly. Then obviously realizing that this casual explanation hardly sounded like a fixed engagement which warranted his absenting himself on Fenella's first night, he added, 'The fact is that one of my friends is to leave for the country tomorrow, and there will be no other opportunity of meeting him.'

'Then you must go, of course,' replied his wife.

'I'll look in on you before I go,' Charlie promised, before going out and closing the door behind him.

There was a short silence, then Dora said with what seemed to Fenella to be forced brightness, 'We shall do much better without him after all. Now do tell me all the news of home. How is everyone? Is Augusta well? Are there any gentlemen interested in her?'

It was quite difficult to give the news from home without mentioning the Grindles, and the possible letting of Yelden Hall. Somehow, though, by concentrating on Mama and Papa and other friends, Fenella managed to do so without sounding as if she was trying to conceal anything. All the same, she was quite relieved when Dora said that it was time for them to change for dinner, so that she could avoid further questioning. Life would be much easier after a day or two, she decided, when once again she and Dora would have shared experiences to reflect upon.

Dinner was a pleasant meal, well chosen and served, and Dora seemed to have settled comfortably into her role as lady of the house.

'In a way, it is easier here than it would have been at Yelden Hall,' she confessed. 'At least here, the servants hired for the season have never known me as anything other than Lady Yelden, whereas at Yelden Hall, I would always fear being compared with Charlie's Mama.'

Fenella, remembering the short, stout figure of the late Lady Yelden, raised her brows and said, 'No really?' which made Dora laugh. Later on in the evening, Fenella ventured to say, 'Mama told me that you had been a little dispirited, Dora. We have both been concerned about you.'

'Yes I have, a little,' Dora admitted. 'It is all so strange here, you see, and it has taken me some time to make friends. Of course, Charlie knows a lot of people already, so he does not really understand how I feel.'

Fenella wrinkled her brow. 'But surely, Charlie's friends must be your friends too?'

'Some of them,' Dora agreed. 'Mrs Maxfield is always pleasant, although I can't say that I really warm to her. But gentlemen tend to make friends with other gentlemen, don't they? And besides, Charlie says that it is not fashionable for a wife to hang on her husband's sleeve. I don't want to let him down by seeming to be too clinging. And of course, there is the baby to look forward to.'

'Oh yes,' exclaimed Fenella delightedly. 'I am to be an aunt! I cannot tell you how thrilled I am.'

'So am I,' answered Dora smiling. 'But I do seem to get tired these days, which means that on those occasions when Charlie wants us to do things together, I am sometimes too weary to go with him, and he gets a little annoyed. But my doctor says that that is normal.'

'For husbands to get annoyed?'

'No, silly! For mothers-to-be to become tired. Charlie isn't annoyed about the baby. He's delighted.'

'Of course he is,' Fenella agreed. 'What husband would not be?' Shortly afterwards, the conversation turned to the projected shopping expedition. But after they had retired, she thought again about some of the things that had been said, and was conscious of a feeling of disquiet. It was difficult to put her finger on exactly what was troubling her, but it seemed to have something to do with the fact that Dora was making all kinds of allowances for Charlie's behaviour, whereas no one, in particular Charlie, appeared to be making any allowance for Dora at all.

CHAPTER SEVEN

After his encounter with Fenella Parrish in the Swan at Hounslow, Giles Beville discovered in himself a marked distaste for the company he was keeping. The four actresses, who had seemed earlier on to be tempting and alluring, now appeared to him to be cheap and tawdry, their gowns over-trimmed, their figures rather too obviously on display.

As he had promised, he went with them all to a nearby house belonging to one of the two other men, Kenneth Brooking by name. After a very short time, however, he made his excuses and left.

One of the actresses, a petite blonde dressed rather more modestly than the other three, wrapped her arms around his neck and kissed him.

'I must be losing my charms, if you can leave my side so easily,' she complained.

He smiled down at her. She was quite lovely, her beauty of a style that normally attracted him, and in other circumstances he would have stayed, but the feeling of restlessness remained.

' 'Tis not your fault, Amelia,' he assured her, kissing her in return. 'But I have business in London which cannot wait.'

Amelia Brough pouted: she was not used to being refused by men. She had set her heart upon having Bev for her next lover from the moment when she had first laid eyes on him.

'You only remembered it after we had arrived at the inn,' she said suspiciously.

'Yes, I did,' he replied, thinking again of Fenella Parrish.

Her eyes narrowed. 'I could return with you,' she suggested. 'Then, when your business is concluded, we could . . . do something else.'

'Your suggestion is a tempting one, but I fear that I would not give my business the proper attention it deserves if I knew that you were waiting for me,' he drawled, with a suave smile. 'You will have a far more amusing time here, I assure you.'

It was on the tip of her tongue to say something about the young woman whom they had seen at the inn, but some instinct urged her to keep quiet on that score, and she merely said, 'Promise me you'll come and see me in London.'

'Need you ask?' he murmured, bowing with his hand on his heart.

His words need not be a lie, he reflected, as he rode away from Brooking's *cottage orné*. He would almost certainly see her treading the boards at Drury Lane, even if he decided against a closer association. True, she was very pretty, but he did not care to be pursued quite so openly. A little more disdain would attract him more.

At once he thought again of Fenella Parrish. As far as beauty alone was concerned, she was not nearly as attractive as her sister Dora, for example. He had flirted with the older Miss Parrish quite as much for his own pleasure as for any other reason, as soon as he had seen her lovely face. But the younger sister had an eager enthusiasm for life, and a determined loyalty to her family which was very engaging. He thought of her expression when she had seen him at the inn. She had eyed him at first with open friendliness, then with disgust. No doubt she did not care for the company he kept, he decided.

It was not surprising. The women of his acquaintance came from two different spheres. Either they were ladies, gently bred, inhabiting the ballrooms, drawing-rooms, assemblies, courts and theatre audiences where he also played his part. Or they were part of the demi-monde; actresses, singers, dancers, who became mistresses of men of rank, and could be found in brothels, green rooms, and in some private houses for entertainments of a very special kind. Only in a few public places, such as Ranelagh, Vauxhall Gardens, or occasionally in Hyde Park, could both groups of the fair sex be found at the same time, carefully keeping out of each other's way for the most part.

But men such as himself moved easily between the two worlds, recognized, acknowledged and even welcomed by both, so long as no attempt was made to bring the two groups together. Bev recalled an acquaintance of his who had, for a bet, introduced an actress into a select musical gathering. His hostess had been so incensed that he had been forced to take himself off to the Continent for a period of time and, after his return, he had only been accepted back into that lady's good graces after he had written her a handsome apology. The actress hadn't been too pleased with him either.

Taking all that into account, it was not surprising that Miss Parrish had turned away so contemptuously. She need not have worried. He might be known as the Wild Marauder, but he knew the rules. He would never have compromised her by acknowledging her whilst he was in such company. What did surprise him, however, was the pleasure that he had felt at the very sight of her. Absurdly, he had found himself suddenly longing that Brooking, Amelia and the others could instantly disappear, leaving him free to greet her and perhaps receive in return the friendly smile that he remembered so well from their previous encounters.

He had been abroad for approximately five years, and since his return to England he had largely busied himself with his estate, but as he rode into the capital, it felt as though he had never been away. The sights, the sounds, the smells were all the same, and he remembered that this was *his* city. It was here where, twenty years ago, he had been introduced to all the amusements that the place could provide, and plunged into them with such abandon that he had earned the nickname by which he was still known. It was here where he had learned to gamble, and discovered the need to restrain himself before he lost every penny he had. It was here where he had had his heart broken for the first time, and the second . . .

Clicking his heels against his horse's sides,

he quickened his pace until he arrived in Half Moon Street where his friend and one-time roistering companion, Lord Richard Byles, had lodgings.

He and Richard had been in the same year at Harrow, and had been friends ever since, going to Oxford together, both having a short career in the army, and then selling out and settling in London.

There the similarity ended however. Bev was a wealthy man without a relation in the world save for Connie Maxfield, his parents both having died when he was in his early twenties. Lord Richard, on the other hand, was the youngest of the Duke of Preston's seven children, all of whom were still living, and he was frequently out of pocket. Despite his hand-to-mouth existence, however, Lord Richard was irrepressibly cheerful, and it was with a feeling of pleasurable anticipation that Bev knocked on the door of his lodgings.

A servant answered the door, but before Bev could even state his business, there was a clatter of footsteps on the stairs and Lord Richard himself appeared, his round cheerful face wreathed in smiles.

'Bev, my dear fellow, I *knew* it was you! I just glanced out of the window to see if it was raining and I saw you below. I'd recognize your seat on a horse anywhere. How are you? What the deuce of a long time you've been away! Have you dined? I'm about to go to Old

Slaughter's for a bite to eat. Are you engaged? Will you come?'

Bev wrung his friend's hand, laughing. 'Which question shall I answer first, I wonder? I'm well. Yes, I have been away a long time, but the Continent is deucedly big to explore, you know. No, I haven't dined, nor am I engaged. But I do have a horse that needs attending to.'

'My man'll take charge of your horse. Are you stabling in the same place as before?' Bev nodded his assent. 'Then it can be taken there for you. See to it, Marshall, will you?' he added to the servant. 'Now come, Bev, let's dine, and you can tell me all your news.'

As they walked the length of Piccadilly, they found plenty to talk about.

'So you have been exploring the Continent,' remarked Lord Richard. 'Did you chance to meet my aunt Mathilde while you were in France?'

'I had the honour of meeting the countess twice,' replied Bev. 'I believe she sent you her greetings. Then I travelled through Italy and as far as Greece.'

'You made a Grand Tour in effect,' laughed Lord Richard. 'Don't you ever get tired of trying to make yourself understood?' Bev laughed, and Lord Richard snapped his fingers. 'Of course, I forget, you're a master of languages!'

'Hardly a master,' replied Bev.

'You're fluent in French and Italian, ain't you?'

'Yes, but my German is very rough, and so is my Greek.'

Lord Richard snorted. 'At least you speak some,' he said frankly. 'So how did you amuse yourself?'

'I visited some old friends in Italy and another in Greece. I took in the sights.'

'And serenaded the ladies?'

Bev inclined his head. 'As you say,' he replied.

Lord Richard thought privately about the lady whose callous rejection had sent Bev fleeing from London, but he said nothing of it, merely commenting, 'Well, I'm deuced glad to see you back. I've missed you Bev. And what's more, London's been devilish dull without the Wild Marauder.'

Bev grinned widely. 'Surely I'm not the only idiot who can entertain everyone by kicking up a dust,' he replied. 'Anyway, enough of me: tell me what you have been getting up to.'

'Now *there's* a story,' replied Lord Richard obligingly. 'Did you hear about how I almost became engaged last year? It was a very narrow squeak, I can tell you.'

Bev had not heard the story and had his own reasons for being glad to change the subject, so he encouraged Richard to tell him of the previous year's exploits. The remainder of the journey was, therefore, spent in Lord

Richard's recounting how a certain lady had made up her mind that he would make her daughter a good husband, and had thenceforward hotly pursued him with such determination that at times he had been almost too fearful to go out.

'So in what form did your rescue come?' Bev asked him as they arrived at Slaughter's.

'In the form of Sir Percy Chilsey,' replied Lord Richard.

'Chilsey! Good heavens! I thought he was dead.'

'So did most of society. He was merely taking the waters at Harrogate, however, and he came back to London in search of a wife.'

'A wife! He must be at least seventy!'

'Sixty-nine, I believe. Anyway, the fair Gwendolen's mama decided that he was a better bet, and so I escaped.'

'Any regrets?' asked Bev curiously.

'Not when I hear her giggle,' replied his friend. 'It's the most appalling sound in the world, and decidedly not something to be endured over the breakfast-table.' With that, both men laughed and walked into the coffee house.

Once inside, they met two other men who were delighted to see Bev, and the four of them made a convivial group over a tasty supper of lamb chops served with potatoes and a fricassee of vegetables.

'What say you to a game of dice, or perhaps

a hand of cards?' suggested one of the men after dinner was over. 'There's a new gaming hell just around the corner.'

Having no commitments, Bev agreed.

'I'll come,' added Lord Richard. 'My pockets are entirely to let until next week when my allowance comes, so I doubt if I'll play myself.'

'Where's the fun in that?' asked the man, who had suggested that they all go.

'Oh believe me, you can't imagine how delightful it is to watch other people lose their money,' replied Lord Richard cheerfully.

'I'll frank you. You might get lucky,' offered the fourth member of the group.

'It's precisely because I never let anyone frank me that I survive from month to month,' replied Lord Richard with unimpaired good humour.

The new hell, Robinson's by name, was already quite full by the time they got there. In one of the rooms, three pairs of gentlemen were engaged in playing piquet, whilst in another, a group was in the midst of a game of faro. From the amount of money and notes of hand that littered the table, it seemed clear that play had been going on for some time and was pretty deep. One of the men thus engaged glanced round at the newcomers.

'Devil take me, it's the Wild Marauder,' he declared. 'When did you return?'

'Well met, Garstone,' replied Bev. 'To

England some months ago; to London, only very recently. Are you winning?'

Garstone laughed derisively. 'Let me see this game out, and you can have my place with the greatest of pleasure,' he declared. The game proceeded and five minutes later he got up from the table. 'Come, Richard, help me drown my sorrows,' he said, clapping Lord Richard on the shoulder. Bev sat down in his place. Glancing round, he saw that the other men at play were all known to him and among them, he spotted Lord Yelden.

'Give you good evening, Yelden,' he said. 'How goes *your* fortune?'

Charlie laughed. 'I don't advise you to play against me,' he said. 'I can't lose tonight.'

But when Bev got up an hour later, taking his modest winnings with him, Charlie was still playing, the mound of coins next to him considerably smaller than it had been earlier.

'Don't worry, I shall come about,' said Charlie cheerfully. 'I know my luck's improving.'

'Young Yelden's dipping deep again,' commented a man in a violet coat, with whom Bev had a slight acquaintance.

'He makes a habit of it, then?' murmured Bev.

The other man nodded. 'Here—or somewhere else,' he replied. 'It's in the blood, of course.'

'Really?' Bev raised his brows.

'Oh yes. His father was a gamester. He had to mortgage Yelden Hall at one time, I believe.'

'Presumably he must have made a recovery,' replied Bev.

'I don't know. But as for Charlie, I understand he's taken measures recently to improve his situation.'

'Really?'

'Yes, I understand he married a fortune. A beauty too, curse his luck! Care for a game of piquet?'

Bev agreed, and for the next hour or so was lost in a game of skill which he particularly enjoyed. But later, as he walked back to his lodgings, he remembered Charlie's avid expression as he waited for the turn of the next card, and he was conscious of a feeling of disquiet. He had seen that expression on the faces of many men, and quite a few of them had come to ruin. Brindle might have heard that Charlie had married a fortune, but Bev knew that in this instance rumour had lied. Dora's fortune had been no more than modest, and was certainly not sufficient to sustain a dedicated gambler for more than a few weeks. Had Charlie dipped into it already, or was the money that he had inherited himself sufficient to sustain his habit?

CHAPTER EIGHT

On her first night in London, Fenella found it virtually impossible to sleep. Quite apart from the various matters which absorbed her thoughts, she was completely unused to being in a place that was not quiet at night. From her room back at Brightstones, she might sometimes hear the call of an owl or a fox or perhaps a nightingale. Here in London, there was always the sound of revelry, sometimes near by, sometimes far distant; footsteps in the street, horses' hooves and the sound of a church clock; and just when it seemed as if she might drop off, the call of someone informing her of the time. Eventually she fell into a fitful sleep, only to be awakened a short time later by the house stirring. When she decided at last to give up trying to sleep and to get up, she felt as if she had never been to bed at all. But some hot chocolate brought to her room by Millie, and the warm water for washing in did much to revive her, and when she had eaten her breakfast she felt much more like her usual self.

'However do you manage to sleep?' she asked Dora at the breakfast table. 'It's like trying to settle in the middle of a fair-ground.'

Dora laughed. 'At first, I felt the same as you,' she said. 'But I soon got used to it.'

'I'm sure I never shall,' replied Fenella fervently. Then after a moment or two she added curiously, 'Do you *like* living in London?'

Dora's face changed. 'To speak confidentially, I don't really like it very much. One always seems to be so very busy, but never doing things that really matter. I am looking forward to the time when my physician says that I can travel, then I shall go back to Yelden Hall. I have so many plans I want to work on.'

'Will Charlie want to go?' Fenella asked her. A slight shadow crossed Dora's face.

'I don't know,' she said. 'I hope so. After all, he is country born and bred, like me. But even if he doesn't want to go there, there is no reason why I should not do so.'

It seemed to Fenella that wherever Charlie might have been born, he was now showing a clear preference for London. It also occurred to her that there had been a time when Dora would have done anything rather than even consider being separated from Charlie once they were married. Rather than give voice to either of these disquieting thoughts, however, she changed the subject.

'Where are we going to do our shopping today?' As she had hoped, this diverted Dora's attention, and soon they were discussing fashions.

When they left the house, there was still no sign of Charlie. Fenella did not ask about him, and Dora did not volunteer any information. Clearly, to have a conversation with a man in whose house she was staying was going to prove to be more difficult than she had supposed.

'If I'm going alone, I usually go in a sedan chair,' Dora confessed later as they rattled through the uneven streets. 'But it's easier with two of us if we go in the carriage, and after all, we may have a lot of parcels to bring home. Besides, if we are together, I can point out any interesting sights, or people of note.'

Certainly Fenella found plenty to look at. Truth to tell, she had been a little too tired to take very much in the previous day, and as she had arrived in Curzon Street a little later than expected, the light had already been going as they entered London. Today however, the day, though cold, was bright and clear and it was much easier to look around. The noise struck her as much as the bustle of the place. Every corner seemed to have its street seller, each one barking out his wares, or advertising his services at the top of his voice. Fenella, snugly wrapped in her cloak of finest broadcloth, her hands kept warm in her sealskin muff, felt very glad that she didn't have to earn her living in a similar fashion.

The modiste's to which Dora led her was in New Bond Street, and Mme Lisette seemed extremely obliging, leading Fenella to think that Dora had probably been there before on her own account. This was confirmed when Dora said, 'This is my sister, Madame, come to stay with me so that I can show her a little town life. She needs some new things as she has only just come from the country.'

'So I see, my lady,' replied Mme Lisette, and Fenella, who had until then felt quite satisfied with her appearance, suddenly felt rather dowdy and provincial. The Frenchwoman eyed her critically.

'Mademoiselle does not have milady's striking beauty,' she said at last, 'but she has a *qualité* all her own which we shall try to capture.' She walked all the way around Fenella, examining her critically, and it was all that Fenella could do to resist pulling at her cuffs or fidgeting with her hair or her ribbons. At last, Madame said, 'Yes, I think that something may be achieved.'

More relieved than she would have thought possible at not being considered a hopeless case, Fenella sat down with Dora, whilst styles, fashions and clothes for every possible time of day were discussed.

Sir Humphrey was a fond and generous father, and he had told her not to stint herself. Even so, Fenella felt a little guilty at the number of gowns that she had ordered, and asked Dora anxiously as they left the shop if she really thought that half as many would be needed.

'Why certainly,' Dora replied. 'It would

never do to keep appearing at functions in the same gown. What a stir that would cause!' She smiled and caught hold of her sister by the arm. 'I'm so glad you have come. This has given me a new lease of life.'

Fenella felt quite sure that they would go home after this, but Dora declared that they must now go on to visit Thomas Jones, a haberdashery situated at Holborn Bridge. 'It is no good, you know, to have a new gown if your shawls, gloves and stockings look worn or old-fashioned. You might as well not bother with the new gown!'

Fenella went willingly enough, for to one who was accustomed to the modest fare that could be provided in Cookham, the opportunity to inspect such a vast array of goods as was available in London under one roof was novelty indeed. But when it came to purchasing new things, she held firm.

'I can understand that a gown may be out of style,' she said. 'But how can that be true of a shawl or a pair of gloves? I certainly need some new stockings, but for the rest, I shall wait until my new gowns come, then bring a small piece of the material to match and buy if necessary.'

Dora could see the sense of this suggestion, but declared that they might as well still go to look at the shop that she had suggested.

'We will at least have an idea of what they have there,' she said. 'And in any case, looking is nearly as enjoyable as buying, I think.'

'I'm quite agreeable,' replied Fenella, 'if you're sure it will not be too much for you.'

'Oh no,' declared Dora robustly. 'I feel as fit as a . . . a . . .'

'Flea?' suggested Fenella. Her sister laughed, and in great good humour, they set out for Holborn. On arrival there, they got out of the carriage, and paused to look in the window of one of the shops, and an acquaintance of Dora's came over to speak to her. Fenella turned away from the display and, as she did so, her eye was caught by something in a shop window on the other side of the street. As she stood looking at it, she became aware that a horseman was slowing to a halt next to her. Looking up, she saw Giles Beville, who touched his hat, inclined his head politely, and looked as if he might approach her. Quite involuntarily her heart gave a leap, but then she remembered how he had ignored her in the inn, so after staring at him for a few moments, she deliberately turned her back without acknowledging him. A few moments later, Dora's acquaintance went on her way, and when Fenella next looked towards the road, Bev had gone. She did not know whether to be glad or sorry. She did not mention the incident to her sister, but if asked would not have found it easy to give a reason for this reticence.

When at last the day's shopping was over

96

and they returned home, Dora looked very tired.

'Why don't you go and lie down on your bed?' Fenella said to her.

'But I don't like to leave you,' Dora protested, not very convincingly.

'Nonsense,' replied her sister. 'I can entertain myself very well, I assure you. I must write to Mama, for one thing, and I might even have a lie down myself.'

'That might be sensible,' agreed Dora. 'We are to go out tonight, so you will want to be rested.'

'I didn't think you'd want to take me out until I was fit to be seen,' replied Fenella with a twinkle.

'As if I should care, when I have my own dear sister with me,' protested Dora. Then in more down-to-earth tones, she added, 'Besides, you and I are the same size—or at any rate we are when I am not increasing. After my rest, we'll go through my wardrobe and find something becoming that no one will remember seeing me in.'

Deciding that she really did not want to sleep, Fenella went to the book-room and sat down to write a letter to her mother. Mama would be glad to hear that Dora was feeling better, she decided. She would also be interested to hear about the shopping expedition. Thinking back to all they had done, Fenella remembered seeing Giles

Beville and recalled, with a pang of guilt, how she had turned her back on him.

'But it was quite his own fault,' she said out loud, angry with herself for feeling guilty. 'He did exactly the same thing to me in Hounslow. He deserves a taste of his on medicine.' Putting all thoughts of the Wild Marauder out of her head, she settled down to write her letter, and had almost finished when the door opened and Charlie looked in.

'I shan't disturb you,' he said, when he saw that she was writing.

Realizing that here was the opportunity that she had been looking for, Fenella laid down her pen carefully and stood up. 'No, don't go away, Charlie. Come in. There was something I wanted to ask you.'

He looked at her warily, but did as she requested, closing the door behind him.

Knowing that there was no easy way of approaching this matter, Fenella said straight away, 'Charlie, when are you going to tell Dora that you are letting Yelden Hall?'

He stepped back defensively. 'What the deuce is it to do with you?' he demanded.

'Nothing at all,' replied Fenella.

'Then mind your own damn business,' he retorted, his face reddening. 'How the devil do you know about it, anyway?'

'It may not be my business, but you cannot deny that it is Dora's,' she said firmly, ignoring the last part of his speech because she did not want to betray Dudley's confidence.

'Dora's my wife, and she'll do as I say,' he said belligerently. Fenella stared at him. It was if she was talking to a stranger, rather than to a young man whom she had known all her life.

'It's not a question of doing as you say,' Fenella replied, trying to be reasonable. 'You could not have a more loyal wife than Dora, and you know it. But she is counting on going to Yelden Hall after the baby is born, and how can she do that if the Hall is let?'

Charlie came towards her, his brow lowering. 'She was perfectly content to be in London before you came,' he said accusingly.

'She is content here because she wants to please you,' Fenella replied, taking a step or two back. 'But she loves the country best, you know that she does.' He was ominously silent, so she went on quickly, 'Charlie, Yelden Hall is yours to do with as you please—'

'I'm glad you admit that, at least,' he sneered.

'. . . but Dora is entitled to hear the news that it is to be let from you and from no one else,' Fenella went on. 'Think how she would feel if she should hear it from another.'

He took a few steps closer to her, and for the first time she began to feel alarmed. 'If I should discover that she has heard about it from you, then I swear you'll regret it,' he said threateningly.

For one brief moment, Fenella wondered

whether he might actually offer her violence, but before he could say or do anything, there was a knock at the door and the butler came in.

'Excuse me, my lord, but her ladyship is awake and is asking for you.'

'I'll go to her,' Charlie replied, but the expression that he cast in his sister-in-law's direction as he left the room was very far from friendly.

*   *   *

It did not prove at all difficult to find a gown amongst Dora's collection that would do for Fenella. Jane Scott had been Dora's maid for several years now, and she knew exactly what would become her mistress's younger sister.

'That primrose silk, my lady, with the cream underdress,' she declared positively. 'It never really became you, but would be much more flattering to Miss Fenella's looks.'

'The very thing!' exclaimed Dora. 'Millie, you can take it and press it, then help my sister dress.'

'Where are we going tonight?' Fenella asked curiously, when the two maids had gone.

'Oh, just to a very small event—a musical evening for a few friends,' replied Dora. 'I confess I prefer the more modest occasions to the very grand ones, and it will mean that when we do go to a ball or assembly of some sort, you will know one or two people already.'

Fenella smiled and agreed, but truth to tell, she had always been more adventurous than Dora and the idea of going to a big event where she might perhaps know nobody at all did not frighten her in the least.

Charlie came downstairs whilst they were standing ready in the hall. He, too, was clearly dressed ready to go out, and he looked at his sister-in-law in a very measuring way. Clearly, he had not spoken to Dora about Yelden Hall, and there was that in his look which unmistakeably threatened Fenella with dire consequences if she were to say anything about the matter to her sister.

Determined not to be cowed by him, she said brightly, 'Are you coming with us tonight, Charlie?' He shot her a look under his brows, but after a moment's indecision seemed to take this comment as a friendly overture, and he made a comically horrified expression.

'One of Lady Appleby's musicales?' he said. 'Good God, no.'

Dora giggled. 'Charlie is not a music lover, are you?' she said.

'I am not, my love, but seeing you looking so delightful almost tempts me.' Dora did indeed look lovely in a gown of deep rose pink, and as Charlie leaned forward to kiss his wife on the cheek, Fenella wondered whether she might have misjudged him. He was, as he had said, under no obligation to explain himself to his sister-in-law, and her words had obviously put him on the defensive. For all Fenella knew, the purpose of letting the hall might be to raise funds in order to prepare some special surprise for his wife.

She was also beginning to realize that the assumptions which she had held concerning marriage did not necessarily apply to couples living in town. Husbands and wives did not seem to live in each other's pockets in London, and Charlie and Dora were obviously no exception to this rule.

Although a small gathering by London standards, Lady Appleby's musicale was quite a large occasion compared with most social events that Fenella had attended. Reluctant though she was to admit it, she began to think that perhaps it was a good idea to be broken in to the London scene in a gentle way.

Lady Appleby was a tall, willowy woman who had clearly had pretensions to beauty in her youth, and who even now could quite truthfully be called a handsome woman. Her ladyship was delighted to meet Lady Yelden's young sister, and very ready to help sponsor Fenella into London society.

'For I have no daughters at all, my dear, and no god daughters either, so it will give me the opportunity which I have always longed for to share in someone's debut.' She turned to Dora. 'Pray tell me if you ever feel too tired to take Miss Parrish about, and I will gladly help if I can.'

'She seems very kind,' said Fenella, after they had left their hostess.

'Yes she is,' agreed Dora, in a low tone. 'But her kindness may not be completely disinterested, I'm afraid. She has one son and is longing for grandchildren, but Nigel seems to be quite happy as a bachelor.' Dora pointed discreetly with her fan to a small group of people who were talking near the fireplace. 'The gentleman in the plum-coloured coat,' she murmured. As if their scrutiny had alerted him to their presence, Lord Appleby looked across at them, excused himself to those with whom he was standing and came over to them.

'Lady Yelden,' he smiled, bowing to Dora. 'And this must be your sister.' Dora agreed that this was so, and introduced them. Looking up from her curtsy, Fenella saw a tall, well-built man, who, although not precisely handsome, had a good-humoured countenance and smiling eyes. He looked to be in his early thirties.

'I trust that you are enjoying your stay in London, Miss Parrish,' he said.

'I have been here for so short a time that I can hardly say as yet,' she confessed. 'But we have been shopping today, have we not, Dora?'

He smiled. 'Ah shopping; the one pursuit which every lady enjoys,' he replied.

'Surely not only ladies,' Fenella responded.

'Everyone likes to have something new, I believe.'

'Very true,' agreed Lord Appleby. 'You put me right, Miss Parrish. But come, allow me to introduce you to some of Mama's other guests.'

Seeing that Dora had now been approached by another acquaintance with whom she was happily exchanging news, Fenella laid her hand on the baron's arm and allowed him to lead her away to rejoin the group by the fireplace, and she was soon playing her part in a lively conversation. By the end of the evening, she could not have told anyone very much about the music that they had heard, which seemed to her in truth to be rather commonplace, but at least she had made some acquaintances whom she would be able to acknowledge on other occasions.

'What did you think of Lord Appleby?' Dora asked her sister with studied casualness as they travelled home.

'He seemed to be very agreeable,' answered Fenella.

'He has a very tidy property in Kent, I believe, although I have never seen it,' Dora went on in the same casual tone.

'Dora, if you are going to start match-making as soon as I arrive, I give you fair warning that I shall go straight home again,' her sister replied, laughing. 'Give me five minutes to settle in, I beg of you!'

'Was I so very obvious?'

'Well, just a little.'

'It's only because I want to do my best for you,' Dora explained. 'Mama would expect it of me.'

'I know she would,' replied Fenella. 'Be assured that when I next write to her I shall tell her that you are introducing me to quantities of gentlemen.'

Dora laughed. 'All right,' she said. 'I will say no more concerning any gentleman's merits. But you won't forget Lord Appleby, will you? I believe him to be most truly the gentleman, and he is spoken well of by everyone.'

'I shan't forget him,' Fenella promised. The conversation ended then, because they had arrived at their own front door, but later on, as she was lying in bed, she thought about what her sister had said. There was no denying that Lord Appleby was a very attractive man. She would be a fool to dismiss him immediately; especially since he appeared to be held in high regard by many. It would be an agreeable change, she told herself firmly, to associate with a man whose character was open for all the world to see.

CHAPTER NINE

Two days later, Dora and Fenella were sitting in the window of the saloon. It was a pleasant room which benefited from the morning sun and both ladies were busy with their needles.

'Do you think that this will be big enough?' Fenella asked her sister, holding up the baby-gown which she had started to make before leaving Brightstones.

'I'm sure it will,' replied Dora. She laid down the bonnet that she was making with a sigh.

'What is it?' Fenella asked her.

'It's just that I can see a time coming quite soon when, because of my condition, I shan't be able to take you out and about very easily. And it is all very well to say that you don't mind, or that Lady Appleby will take you to this and that because I know that she will, and other ladies will help as well, but I don't want to miss it, Nella.' Fenella put down her sewing and took hold of her sister's hand.

'Believe me, I don't want anyone else to take me about except you,' she said. 'But you must think of baby; besides, I will tell you all about everything I do, right down to the very last detail.'

Dora smiled. 'I know that I must keep well because of baby,' she replied, 'and because of that I am resigned to staying in London.' She looked down at their clasped hands for a moment, then looked up at her sister and said, 'Nella, why did you not tell me that Charlie was going to let Yelden Hall?'

'Oh Dora, I'm sorry,' replied Fenella apologetically. 'I didn't know what to do for the best. But it did not seem right for anyone to tell you except Charlie himself.'

'I suppose you are right,' agreed Dora. 'And of course, I understand that he wants me to stay in town near to Dr Driver. It is quite true that since we cannot go back to Yelden Hall, it might as well be earning money for our future, and for its own.' She looked down at her hands again. 'Charlie told me that his father took out a mortgage on the Hall, and that it needs to be paid back,' she explained. 'I do not perfectly understand it, but apparently it means that the Hall is not completely ours until the debt is paid.'

'Does Papa know about this?' Fenella asked her.

Dora shook her head. 'Charlie did not want him to because he was afraid that he might not let us marry. But it is not Charlie's fault, and I do not see why he should be blamed for his father's mistake. If the Hall is let, Charlie says, then the money to pay off the mortgage will soon be raised.'

'What will Charlie say if Papa asks him why he has let Yelden Hall?' Fenella asked.

'I think that he will say that he does not want it to remain unoccupied during the winter months. But Nella, I do not like the idea of not being able to just decide to go there, and then do so—if you see what I mean.' Her voice caught on a sob, and Fenella seized hold of her hands again.

'Would you like me to ask Mama if we can both go to Brightstones?' she asked. 'I know she would be delighted to see you.'

'Yes, she would,' agreed Dora. 'And it is lovely to know that I can always go there if I need to do so, but Charlie wants me to stay here, and I must not go against his wishes. Maybe later, he'll let me go to Yelden Hall, after the people have gone.'

Fenella found herself remembering how four years ago a bad harvest had caused some difficulties for her father and his tenants. The reason why this stayed in her mind was because her father had not travelled with them to visit friends that year, but had remained to tend his acres. They had all missed him, but he had remained adamant that his duty required him to stay on his own land. She knew that she had little experience of farming matters, and even less of financial ones, but she could not help wondering whether a man in Charlie's circumstances was really wise to reside in such an expensive place as London. It also occurred to her that having made the decision to let the Hall, Charlie would be unlikely to ask his tenants to vacate within the foreseeable future. She kept these thoughts to herself, however, and instead she held up the tiny garment that she was sewing and said, 'Do you think I should embroider anything on these sleeves, or leave them plain?'

Dora was just considering her answer when the door opened and the butler announced Mrs Maxfield, Miss Maxfield and Mr Beville.

Much to her annoyance, Fenella could feel herself flushing. There was no earthly reason why she should feel embarrassed, she told herself. It was he who had ignored her first, after all. That being the case, Beville should surely be the one to be embarrassed. It was therefore difficult to explain why she should be feeling unsettled in his presence, whereas he, bowing urbanely, and clad in a superbly cut coat of dark-blue brocade, appeared to be completely at ease.

Dora came forward to greet the visitors in her usual composed way, but Fenella, very sensitive to her sister's moods at present, thought that she could detect a slight hesitation in her manner. It made her wonder whether she had heard of Bev's reputation and would have preferred not to receive him.

Mrs Maxfield came hurrying forward in a cloud of scent, both hands held out. 'Lady Yelden! My dear, you are blooming! It is not hard to guess why, of course. You have a delightful visitor, I can see.'

'Mrs Maxfield, how do you do?' Dora replied, giving her hands to her visitor. Fenella, noticing her slight hesitation, recalled that Dora had always been rather reserved with everyone apart from her family and those she knew very well. 'How good of you to come. I was intending to call upon you myself very soon. I gather that you remember my sister.'

'Certainly I remember Miss Parrish very well indeed,' replied Mrs Maxfield, smiling warmly. She was looking very handsome in a gown of bronze velvet with a matching bonnet. 'Have you only just arrived in London, Miss Parrish?'

'Only a few days ago,' Fenella replied.

'You must be pleased to see your sister looking so well.'

Fenella nodded in agreement. 'Mama will be very relieved to hear a good report of her,' she said.

'Mothers do worry,' agreed Mrs Maxfield. 'I am constantly having to send reports of my sister-in-law to her mama. You remember my sister, Miss Parrish?' Fenella acknowledged that she did. 'And perhaps you also remember my cousin, Mr Beville.'

Fenella had to remind herself that as far as the other three ladies in the room were concerned, she had only met Bev twice, once briefly on the dance floor, and then again at Dora's wedding.

'Yes, I think I do just remember Mr Beville,'

110

she replied, wrinkling her brow as if to recall his face were a real effort.

He inclined his head, his hand on his heart. 'Whereas I have carried your memory with me ever since, Miss Parrish,' he replied with a twinkle.

'Are you sure that you are not confusing me with some other lady?' she asked him demurely, 'there being doubtless so many.' Dora looked a little shocked, but Bev laughed out loud.

'Your qualities are far too remarkable for that, ma'am,' he replied.

The Maxfields stayed for only a few more minutes, but in that time, an arrangement was made for the two groups to go to the theatre together.

'Have you ever been to the theatre, Miss Parrish?' Mrs Maxfield asked her.

Fenella had to admit that she had not. 'I have seen plays performed in private,' she admitted, 'and at the fair once, but I have never been to the play.'

'You will enjoy it enormously, I know,' said Mrs Maxfield. 'You will persuade Lord Yelden to come, won't you?' she went on, addressing Dora. 'I shall try to get Maxfield to come with us, but he is no great lover of drama.'

'Nor is Charlie,' confessed Dora. 'But I shall do my best.'

'Well if they won't come, we shall just have to share Bev between us,' answered his cousin gaily.

After she had gone, Fenella declared, 'Share him! She can have my portion and welcome.' Immediately she regretted her words, for Dora looked at her in some surprise.

'What is the matter with you, Nella?' she asked. 'You have only met him twice and that some time ago, but the first thing that you did when he arrived today was to flirt with him in a very strange way. Now you seem to have developed some kind of animosity towards him. What is the reason for your attitude?'

Fenella was so accustomed to giving the lead to her gentle sister, even though she was the younger, that it seemed strange to realize that here in London, Dora as a married woman was responsible for her, and answerable to Mama for her conduct.

She shrugged her shoulders. 'I don't know,' she replied. 'But I have heard tell that he is something of a . . . a rake.'

Dora frowned. 'He certainly was one before he left this country, although his cousin swears that he has reformed. But where did you hear this gossip? From someone at Lady Appleby's house last night?'

'It must have been,' replied Fenella. Then fortunately, before her sister could interrogate her further, Lord Appleby himself was announced and he came in, bowing and smiling.

'It is such a fine day, that I wondered whether you would like to come driving with me this afternoon?' he asked Fenella.

Dora nodded. 'Yes, do go, Nella,' she said. 'I shall be glad of the chance to lie down on my bed.'

Dora's wardrobe was raided yet again as soon as Lord Appleby had gone, and Jane Scott soon brought out a separate bodice and skirt in a rich russet, and a velvet pclisse of a darker shade. Fenella could not help feeling a little guilty at wearing Dora's lovely things, but Jane reassured her.

'Her ladyship's got plenty of clothes and she won't miss these.' Consequently, when Lord Appleby arrived, Fenella felt that she looked her best, and his admiring expression assured her that she was not mistaken in this feeling.

His lordship was driving a fine pair of chestnut horses harnessed to his curricle, and Fenella, who had been taught to drive by her father, was impressed by his skill. He had light hands and sought to give her a comfortable ride, rather than demonstrate how many risks he could take, as some of their younger neighbours in Berkshire were inclined to do. The favourable impression that she had gained of him so far was confirmed, and she was soon chatting happily to him about her life in the country, and her impressions of London so far.

'Do you want to view the sights of historic interest while you are here, or do you despise such activities?' he asked her.

Fenella wrinkled her brow. 'I am not quite sure how I should answer that,' she replied. 'You give me the impression that to despise such activities is the fashionable thing to do, and I have no wish to be thought dowdy.'

'There is no danger of that, dressed so becomingly as you are,' he replied gallantly. 'And yet I suspect from *your* answer that you are by no means uninterested in monuments of the past.'

'I do confess it,' agreed Fenella, her colour a little high from his compliment. 'What is to be done?'

'I suggest that you make a point of viewing exactly what you want to see whenever you want to do so, and that on such occasions you dress in the height of fashion and travel as ostentatiously as you can contrive. Who knows, you might even set a new style?'

'I doubt it,' she retorted. 'But I shall certainly go and visit the places that interest me.'

'You will need someone to go with you,' he pointed out.

'No doubt someone will take pity on me,' she said lightly. 'I suppose I could even drive myself to some of the places that I want to see. Would that be ostentatious enough, my lord?'

He frowned slightly. 'Perhaps a little too much so,' he replied. 'I cannot say that I approve of females driving. But if I can take you anywhere, please consider me at your service.' She thanked him, but then turned the conversation to other matters. She liked him very well, although she found his attitude to ladies' driving somewhat old-fashioned. Nevertheless, she had no wish, as yet, to invite any attentions from him that were out of the ordinary.

When they arrived back at the house, Fenella invited him in for some refreshment. He accepted, and when they got inside, they found that Dora had risen from her bed, having had a refreshing sleep. She was very pleased to welcome Lord Appleby, and Fenella was not sorry when her sister invited him to join them for their evening at the theatre. It would give her a chance to see how he conducted himself in another setting.

By the time the outing to the theatre took place, some of Fenella's new gowns had arrived, and she was able to wear something entirely of her own choice, rather than something which had first been chosen by her sister for herself. It was of a pale mauve, with a cream petticoat embroidered with mauve and yellow flowers, and Fenella liked it more than anything she had yet worn in London.

Charlie, who had agreed to accompany them more willingly than expected that evening, opened his eyes wide when he saw her, and told her that he had never seen her look so well. Fenella smiled her thanks, but could not help wondering whether, in view of the difference of opinion they had had, his remarks were entirely sincere. Dora looked pleased to have Charlie with them, but Fenella thought that she looked a little tired, and wondered whether she might be obliged to withdraw from her engagements sooner than expected.

It had been arranged that the Maxfields, together with Bev and Lord Appleby, would all come and dine, and that they would travel on to the theatre together. Mr and Mrs Maxfield and Miss Maxfield were the first to arrive, and Lord and Lady Yelden both greeted them, Charlie with warmth, and Dora with courtesy. Charlie seemed to be in particularly high spirits, and he made Mrs Maxfield laugh by raising his brows and kissing her hand in an openly flirtatious manner.

'You are a dreadful play-actor,' she declared, rapping him across the knuckles with her fan. 'Is not your husband a play actor, Lady Yelden?'

'Sometimes he is,' replied Dora with a slight smile. Fenella remembered that she had never found flirtation comfortable, either to participate in, or to witness.

Lord Appleby and Giles Beville arrived at the same time. Seeing Bev in his purple satin coat and once more in his paint and powder, Fenella had to remind herself that this was the same man with whom she had chatted so easily

116

at the folly at Brightstones. Lord Appleby, too, looked very elegant, but somehow, next to Bev, he seemed a little dull. She tried to repress the thought, but once it had surfaced it refused to go away.

Dora had ordered a simple meal for them all, since they needed to leave for the theatre soon after they had eaten, and it was a merry party that sat down at the table. Fenella found herself placed between Mr Maxfield and Lord Appleby, both of whom seemed very ready to pay her a flattering amount of attention. She soon realized that she did not much care for Mr Maxfield's style of flirtation, which she found rather bold, especially since she was seated opposite his wife. Mrs Maxfield did not appear to be bound by any similar constraints, however, and flirted animatedly with Bev on her right, then with Charlie on her left.

For his part, Bev seemed to enjoy this attention as much as any man, but he did not allow it to prevent him from paying the proper amount of attention to Miss Maxfield. With her, Fenella noticed, he seemed to be altogether more restrained in his manner, and when she spoke, he gave her his full attention.

Dora, in her place at the foot of the table, appeared to be very calm and at ease. Lord Appleby on her right seemed to understand her dislike of dalliance, and instead talked to her about his country estate, which as a topic suited her much more.

When they were all ready to go, Charlie sent for his carriage, for although the Maxfields had come in theirs, the party was too large for them all to travel together. Fenella felt sure that Dora would be happiest travelling with her husband and sister, but before she could state any preference, Mrs Maxfield declared in lively tones, 'We must mix our party up, Lady Yelden! We cannot possibly be so provincial as to travel with our own husbands! So domestic! Charlie and Bev can come with me in our carriage, and we will take your sister as well. Then our parties will be mixed together as much as possible, I think.'

Fenella would rather have travelled with her sister, but did not want to seem lacking in confidence, so she made no objection to the scheme. The gentlemen sat with their backs to the horses, and Mrs Maxfield chattered in a spirited manner throughout. Occasionally, she applied to Fenella with such remarks as 'I appeal to you, Miss Parrish', or 'Miss Parrish do you not think so?' but otherwise, for the most part, she managed to carry the majority of the conversation. By the time they reached the theatre Fenella had become heartily sick of the sound of her voice; the journey had served to show her that Mrs Maxfield knew both men well, and probably knew Charlie better than she knew Bev.

The theatre in Drury Lane was an impressive sight. There had been a theatre on the site for over a hundred years. The first one had burned down in 1672, having survived the great fire, but it had been rebuilt by Sir Christopher Wren. Since Garrick had established his reign there, the gallery had been enlarged, some of the boxes had been given a new entrance, and the seating capacity had been more than doubled.

There was quite a press of persons entering the theatre and Fenella looked anxiously around for her sister, afraid that she might become crushed. She hoped that Mr Maxfield would make sure that she got to their box safely. She herself was obliged to lean on Mr Beville's arm, and she had to admit that she felt very safe in his masterful care.

To Mr Beville, this was clearly not a new experience, and he even took the opportunity to say ironically, 'Alone at last! I have been wanting to speak to you privately.'

'Privately!' exclaimed Fenella, laughing despite herself. 'How can you be so absurd?'

'Do you really think that anyone will be able to pay any attention to anyone else's conversation here?' he asked her. Then, before she could reply, he went on, 'Why did you cut me in Bond Street the other day?'

She looked at him incredulously for a moment before replying, 'For much the same reason as you ignored me at the inn in Hounslow, I should imagine.'

He chuckled. 'I don't think so,' he returned,

'for you were accompanied by your sister, I believe.'

'Yes, that is so,' she answered in puzzled tones, 'but—'

'My dear Miss Parrish, I hope you will not tell me that there would be any impropriety in your speaking to me whilst accompanied by your sister.'

'No, of course not,' she said, 'but . . .' This time he did not interrupt her. She stopped of her own volition, colouring deeply.

'Precisely, Miss Parrish,' he murmured.

'You mean that they were . . . were . . .'

'Not my sisters? I think we both know what I mean.'

'Well you should not have been consorting with them at all,' she whispered crossly, as they reached the box.

'Perhaps not, but would you have had me compound my error by introducing them to you?'

There was no time for them to say more, for by now they had reached their box and met up with the rest of their party, and as they took their places, she was left undecided as to whether she thought the better or the worse of him for his admission.

Fenella had never before been in a building that held more than 2,000 people, and as she gazed at the splendid decorations conceived by the Adam brothers, and the dazzling array of fashions, she hardly knew what to look at next.

As the time drew near for the play to commence, she was conscious of a sense of mounting excitement, but as the performance began, she found herself torn between enjoyment of the evening and exasperation with those around her. The production was a fine one, for they were fortunate enough to see Sarah Siddons taking the leading role in *The Fatal Marriage*. The famous actress commanded immediate respect, but although there was a palpable silence when she was on stage, at other times it was quite difficult to concentrate, however, because of the noise and activity generated by the audience.

Finding Mr Beville sitting next to her, Fenella turned to him at one point and exclaimed, 'Does no one come here to watch the play?'

He grinned. 'Very few, I fear. Although, as you see, Siddons can command silence, most of the time the audience are here to see and be seen.'

'But why not wait until the interval?' Fenella asked him.

'Ah, but if they did so, they would waste precious minutes deciding upon whom they should pounce. This way, as soon as the interval commences, everyone can leap up out of his seat and make a rush for the person of his choice.'

'And where will you be rushing to, Mr Beville?' she asked him, because she could not resist.

His eyes twinkled. 'I? But why should I be rushing anywhere when my quarry is here, Miss Parrish?'

'Here, sir?'

'Can you doubt it?' he murmured, inclining his head.

She turned back towards the stage, but it must be confessed that it was several minutes before she could really concentrate on the play.

As soon as the interval began, Mr Maxfield excused himself, and Lord Appleby escorted Miss Maxfield out of the box. True to his word, Mr Beville did not disappear, but offered Fenella his arm so that they might walk about a little. She turned to her sister enquiringly, but Dora said cheerfully, 'You go so that Mr Beville may show you a little more of the theatre. Charlie and I will stay here together like an old married couple.'

Charlie looked anything but pleased at this suggestion, and he turned to Dora and said, 'You will be quite safe here, my dear. Connie would like to promenade a little, would you not?'

Thus appealed to, Mrs Maxfield agreed that she would indeed like a little exercise. 'But do not think that I am unaware of a wife's prior claim,' she went on. 'I can very well go with Bev and Miss Parrish.'

'By no means,' declared Charlie. 'I wouldn't

be so ungallant. You'll be quite happy here, won't you, Dora?'

'Of course,' replied his wife immediately, but Fenella thought that perhaps some of the enjoyment went from her sister's face.

Seeing that the other members of the party were leaving the box, or had already left it, Fenella said impulsively, 'Then I will stay with you, Dora. I find no great longing for exercise after all, and will be glad if you will point out some of the notables for me.'

Dora smiled. 'I'll do my best, but I fear I'm still rather ill-informed with regard to persons of note,' she confessed.

Bev, who had risen to escort Fenella, stepped forward. 'Then allow me to lend my expertise,' he said. 'I'll order wine for us, then I'll point out who everyone is, whom you should meet, and whom you should avoid.'

Bev did indeed seem to know most of those who were present, at least by sight, and discoursed so amusingly about the different personalities that Dora and Fenella could not help laughing at his absurdities. Shortly before the interval was over, Fenella looked across to the other side of the theatre, and saw Charlie with Mrs Maxfield in another box. They were talking animatedly with the two ladies who occupied it, and without knowing why, Fenella became conscious of a feeling of disquiet.

By the time the farce had begun, the party had reassembled in the box. There were clearly many people present who had come to watch the farce rather than the serious piece, and it also became obvious that some of the gentlemen were watching the stage with particularly close attention. As the play proceeded, Fenella found that her attention was caught by an actress who was playing the part of an insolent maidservant. Glancing at Bev, she saw him raise his quizzing glass and realized that his interest was similarly caught. Looking down at the stage again, she saw the actress appear to direct a saucy glance in the direction of their box, and at that moment Fenella recognized her. She had been amongst the group that she had seen at the Swan at Hounslow. No wonder Bev had not wanted to acknowledge her!

After the performance was over, they made ready to leave, but before they could do so, a servant came to their box with a note, which he gave to Bev.

'By your leave,' he said, before opening it. It was evidently a very brief note, for it only took him a moment or two to master its contents before he tucked it in the broad cuff of his coat and said to the servant, 'Thank you, there is no answer.'

They made their way out of the theatre, but when they reached the coach, Bev excused himself, pleading another engagement. As they drove off, Fenella wondered whether the note had been from the actress, and whether he had gone to join her even now.

CHAPTER TEN

Fenella thought about the theatre visit for a long time afterwards. There were many reasons for this. For one thing, the performance of Sarah Siddons had been remarkable. The visit to London would have been worthwhile for that alone. For another, the bustle and excitement of the whole event had been very much to Fenella's taste, for, unlike her sister, she enjoyed town life. But one of the things that gave her pause for much thought was the way in which Bev had behaved, and the way in which people had reacted to him. It had become clear that not only did he know all the notables in town, but that he was also something of a celebrity himself. Many had acknowledged him as they had made their way to and from the box, and also whilst they had been seated in it. In addition, Fenella had noticed that speculative glances had been cast at him by some of the ladies present. To add to all of this was the incident of the note, swiftly followed by Bev's excusing himself from their party.

These matters put together gave rise to a thought which she voiced to him two days later when he came to take her for a drive. He arrived punctually at eleven, dressed for driving in a russet brown greatcoat with his hair neatly tied back and unpowdered. Altogether, he looked so much as she remembered him from their first meeting that she was emboldened to speak to him frankly.

'You must think me quite a fool, Mr Beville,' she said, after they had driven a short way.

'By no means,' he replied, in accents which showed his surprise. 'Why should you suppose such a thing?'

'When I first met you, I asked you to flirt with my sister,' she explained.

'It was an unusual request, but not beyond my powers, I believe,' he replied tranquilly.

'But that is precisely what I mean,' she declared. 'You knew how experienced you were in the ways of society, but I did not. I simply thought that you were a . . . a . . .'

'Well?' he pressed her.

'A travel-weary indigent gentleman,' she concluded, in rather a small voice. He laughed, but not unkindly.

'That was rather how I felt at the time, I assure you,' he replied. 'But your request caught my interest and soon I found myself fascinated by the whole business.'

It was on the tip of her tongue to ask him whether he had really been fascinated by the intrigue of it all, or by Dora's beauty, but she stopped herself from giving voice to her suspicion just in time. Not only would such a question be an intolerable impertinence, but also she had suddenly realized that she did not want to hear his answer.

He did not seem aware of any awkwardness in her demeanour, however, and he was soon pointing out to her some of the people who were also taking the air at this time. Fenella only gave his discourse half her attention. She was thinking about how at the theatre Charlie had been so willing to oblige another woman in preference to his wife, and about how readily Bev had sat down to bear herself and Dora company. Yet, from what she had observed since her arrival in London, their behaviour was not unusual. Husbands and wives frequently seemed to attend different functions and meet only by chance, spending most of their time flirting desperately with others. To Fenella, with the examples of her mama and papa and of Rev and Mrs Sandys before her, it seemed a strange way of carrying on.

Without weighing her words first, she said, 'Does no one in London take marriage seriously?'

Bev, who had been in the middle of pointing out Lady Grimley, glanced at her keenly. 'Now, what brought that on?' he asked her.

She coloured. 'Oh, nothing really. I was just thinking.' He waited patiently, and was rewarded when after, a few moments' silence, she went on. 'I suppose I always imagined that Charlie and Dora would settle down at Yelden Hall and be near us and live happily ever after.'

He smiled. 'Everyone does not care for the country,' he replied. 'Plenty of people live very happily in the town, you know.'

'Yes, but not Dora,' replied Fenella positively. 'She has always been a country mouse.'

He paused in thought for a moment, then said gently, 'You forget that she has been married for some months, now. Her tastes may well have changed, to match Lord Yelden's.'

Fenella shook her head vigorously. 'But that is what makes it all so strange,' she said anxiously. 'Until quite recently, I would have said that Charlie was a person who preferred the country as well. But when he came to our house that day—a few days before you arrived—he looked like an elegant stranger. Then he let the Hall without telling Dora about it first . . .' She bit her lip. 'I should not have said that!' she said anxiously. 'Oh pray, sir, do not divulge it.'

'You can rely upon my discretion, Miss Parrish,' he said. 'Is it known why your brother-in-law has let Yelden Hall?'

She was silent for a time, then said in troubled tones, 'I believe that it was mortgaged by Charlie's father. I think that Charlie wants to pay off the mortgage. But . . .' She bit her

128

lip, and looked up at him. He had brought his carriage to a halt and was looking down at her, listening attentively. Suddenly she wanted to confide in him completely, to tell him all her concerns about Dora's distress, Charlie's unreasonable anger, and his insistence on remaining in such an expensive place as London. But she had known him for such a short time, and he was Mrs Maxfield's cousin, and the Wild Marauder to boot, and she feared that she had already said too much.

He glanced down at her serious face as she looked up at him, and his heart was touched. 'You need tell me no more,' he said. 'Naturally you are anxious, but I fear there is not a great deal that you can do. Charlie is a grown man after all. The one thing in your power is to lift your sister's spirits, and that I can see you have already done.'

'You are very kind,' said Fenella in a subdued tone.

'Nonsense,' he returned. 'Just ingratiating myself with a pretty woman, you know.' He paused briefly. 'There may be a perfectly reasonable explanation for why Charlie is letting the Hall. It's one way of making sure that a property is cared for.' He paused again, then went on in a different tone, 'Tell me, Miss Parrish, have you ever learned to drive?'

'Why yes,' she replied, her face lightening. 'Papa taught me, but I've never driven in London.'

He drew his pair to a halt. 'Then now is your chance. Would you like to take a turn with the ribbons?' he asked her, suiting his action to his words.

'You don't think it an unladylike pursuit, then?' she asked him, thinking of Lord Appleby.

'By no means.'

'Are you sure I won't overturn you?'

'I am sure you will excel in this, as you appear to do in everything you attempt,' he responded gallantly.

Fenella was a little nervous at first, for Bev handled his horses superbly, and she was afraid that he might be critical of her efforts. But having handed her the ribbons, he sat back with the air of a man very much at his ease, and that helped her to relax. Soon she forgot her anxieties and simply enjoyed herself, not realizing how much Bev's gaze lingered upon her as she concentrated on her task, bright-eyed and eager.

He took the horses from her in order to drive back through the streets, and when they arrived at Curzon Street, he handed the reins to his groom, so that he could help her down and escort her to the door. Briefly she hesitated, on the point of asking him to keep an eye on Charlie. Then she recalled that this man, too, was a gambler, and an associate of actresses. He would hardly take her anxieties seriously.

*   *   *

After they had parted company later and he had driven his curricle back to the stables, he walked round to his lodging, his face grim. He had seen Charlie gambling on a number of occasions since the night of his arrival. That was not of itself unusual, for after all, he had only seen the young earl because he had been going out to gamble himself. But now that he came to reflect upon the matter, he recalled that Charlie had usually already been present when he arrived, and was often still deeply absorbed in a game when he got up to leave. Furthermore, he never seemed to break off in order to enjoy a drink or conversation. His sole interest in the clubs to which he went seemed to be the gambling, and when he was sitting at table there was on his face an expression of avid interest, as if nothing else mattered save the cards or the dice in his hand. Upon reflection, Bev found this rather disquieting.

This became doubly disturbing, however, coupled with the news that the Hall was let, and also mortgaged. He now recalled hearing someone telling him recently that Charlie's father had been a gambler. Clearly, the late Lord Yelden had mortgaged his home in order to raise money to pay gambling debts. Of course it was admirable that Charlie should

131

wish to pay off the mortgage, but nothing in his manner had so far conveyed to Bev that here was a man anxious to retrench. He would have done much better to take his wife back to Yelden Hall, save on the expense of hiring a house in London, and seek to live modestly whilst caring for his estate.

Taking this into account, Bev could think of only one reason why Charlie might want to let his home. Yelden Hall had belonged to the family for six generations, but Bev had known other men take similar steps. Almost invariably, it had been because they had incurred serious gaming debts. One of them, he recalled, had later hanged himself.

Bev was halfway to his lodging when he stopped and almost shook himself. Lord Yelden was a man whom he barely knew and did not really like very much. His wife, a beautiful creature it was true, was someone with whom he had flirted once, and whom he thereafter had met on a handful of social occasions. Why, then, was he distressing himself with anxieties concerning their financial arrangements? He could think of no clear answer to this question, but when he tried to dismiss the matter from his mind, all he could see was Miss Fenella Parrish's anxious face.

CHAPTER ELEVEN

'Dora, do we really have to go to that wretched concert this evening?' Fenella asked her sister. She had now been in London for long enough for the novelty of going out every night to have palled a little.

The concert to which they had been invited was being given by Mrs Palgrave, a rather depressing woman who furnished her house with drab curtains and carpets and uncomfortable chairs, and then filled it with uninspiring company. Neither of them wanted to attend, but they had been invited by Lady Appleby, and Dora was determined that they should do everything possible to please her.

'You know you like Lord Appleby,' Dora went on. 'And you cannot deny that he would do very well for you. When I retire from the social scene, you will need someone to take you about. Lady Appleby has already expressed her willingness to help, and it will not do to risk offending her.'

Fenella agreed, but only half-heartedly. The last thing she wanted was for Dora to over-exert herself, but the truth was that she did not feel drawn to Lord Appleby in any special way. She had liked him at first, and she still did, but only as a friend. There was nothing about him that made her pulses quicken.

She got ready with Millie's help, putting on an open robe of sky blue with a petticoat of a lighter shade trimmed with silver ribbons. It was whilst Millie was putting the finishing touches to her hair that Dora came into her room, a puzzled look on her face.

'Nella, I didn't lend you my pearl necklace, did I?' she asked.

Fenella started to shake her head, but realizing in time that this would cause problems for Millie, she simply said, 'No, you didn't. I have pearls of my own, don't you remember? You have the ones belonging to Grandma Parrish, and mine were Grandma Lyttleton's.'

'Oh yes, of course,' replied Dora. She was dressed in a gown of dull gold with a cream petticoat. It was cunningly cut to disguise her pregnancy, but those who knew her well would be able to detect the difference in her figure. 'It is just that they would go so well with this gown, and I had made up my mind to wear them. I cannot think where they can have got to.'

'Has your maid taken them to be cleaned, perhaps?' suggested Fenella.

'That was the first thing I thought of, but she says that she has not,' answered Dora. 'Besides, Mama had all my jewellery cleaned and the clasps checked before I got married.' She sighed. 'I suppose they will turn up in the wrong box, or hidden under something else.'

'But meanwhile, you do not have them to wear,' said Fenella. 'You may borrow mine, if you like. Millie, get them out, please.'

'No, Nella, I couldn't possibly,' protested Dora. 'I'll wear some other jewels.'

'It ought to be pearls with that gown,' said Fenella critically. 'Besides, I am wearing the sapphire pendant that Papa gave me for my sixteenth birthday, so I shan't need them tonight.' Seeing that her sister still looked reluctant, she leaned forward and clasped her hand impulsively. 'Do say that you will! You have given me so many of your gowns. It will be just like old times—sharing each other's things.'

'Oh, all right,' Dora said eventually, smiling. 'Thank you, Nella. I will take the greatest care of them.'

Fenella helped her to clasp them around her neck, and they went downstairs together. Charlie was at the bottom of the stairs, dressed for the evening in a blue satin coat, and he smiled up at them as they came downstairs.

'Are you dining with us, Charlie?' Dora asked him hopefully.

'If you will permit,' he said, bowing gallantly. Then, as he straightened, he added, 'Upon my soul, you two ladies look . . .' He stopped short, his eyes drawn to Dora. 'Your pearls,' he said involuntarily, then stopped again, biting his lip.

'No, they're not mine,' said Dora. 'They're

Nella's. Really, it is very vexing. I cannot find mine at all, and they are such a fine string from Grandma Parrish. I dare say they will turn up.'

'Oh, did I not say?' said Charlie casually, his eyes not quite meeting hers as he spoke. 'I thought the string looked a little stretched and weak last time you wore them, so I have taken them to the jeweller's to have them restrung for you.'

Dora wrinkled her brow. 'Restrung? But that was done just before we were married, less than a year ago. They felt quite all right to me the last time I wore them.'

'But they did not look right to me,' replied Charlie, in a tone that was almost patronizing. 'Really, my dear, you must allow me to know best in this matter.'

Fenella opened her mouth to say that if anyone would know if pearls needed restringing it must surely be the woman who clasped them around her neck, but she closed it again. She did not want to appear to take sides in a disagreement between husband and wife.

'It just surprises me,' said Dora. 'It was Bennet's in Maidenhead who did it. They have always looked after our jewels, and—'

'Well they evidently didn't do it properly on this occasion,' said Charlie. His voice had an edge to it this time.

'I understand your making such a decision,'

said Dora placatingly, 'even if I don't think that it was necessary. But why did you not tell me? Jane has been looking all over for my pearls, and no doubt blaming herself for losing sight of them, and she could have been saved the trouble and worry if you had only said something.'

Charlie flushed. 'Upon my word, I will seek to oblige your maidservant more on another occasion! I took time and trouble to have your pearls cleaned and restrung, but I shan't bother another time, if this is all the thanks I get.' He walked to the door then turned round, his hand on the handle. 'I've changed my mind about dinner: I shall dine at my club, where hopefully the company will be less critical.'

Dora took a step or two towards him, stretching out her hand. 'Charlie,' she said.

He stared at her coldly. 'I wish you both a pleasant evening,' he said, bowing almost imperceptibly, and left.

'Charlie . . .' Dora murmured again, after the door had slammed behind him.

Fenella put an arm around her sister's shoulders. 'Come and sit down for a few minutes and compose yourself,' she said, anxious to get her away from curious eyes. 'It isn't quite dinner-time yet.'

When they were in the saloon with the door closed, Dora turned to Fenella and said 'Nella, do you think I was being unfair?'

A few minutes before, Fenella had

137

remained neutral, but Dora was her sister after all. 'No, I don't,' she replied decisively. 'I don't want to seem critical of Charlie, but he should have told you. For all he knew, you might have dismissed one of the servants by now for theft.'

Dora sighed. 'Yes I know,' she agreed. 'But he dines at home so seldom. It seems a pity to anger him on one of the few occasions when he had intended to do so.'

They were about to go in to dinner when the front door bell rang, and moments later, the door opened to admit Dudley Sampson and his sister Augusta. They were accompanied by a young man whom Fenella recognized as being Simon Grindle.

'Forgive us for appearing at such an hour, but we have just arrived in London and we had to come and see you straight away,' said Augusta, hurrying to kiss Dora, then Fenella.

'The hour is of no consequence,' exclaimed Dora, her eyes very bright as she greeted both Augusta and Dudley.

Fenella could see that the unexpected pleasure of meeting old friends coming so soon after her disagreement with Charlie was threatening to overcome her, so she said quickly, 'What's more, you give us an excellent excuse for crying off from an engagement that we both wanted to avoid.'

'You are looking well—both of you,' said Dudley. 'But Dora, you must allow me to introduce Mr Simon Grindle to you.'

138

Simon bowed, saying, 'It's a pleasure to meet you, Lady Yelden. I do trust that you do not feel that my presence here is an intrusion.' On the surface, he was simply referring to the fact that he, a stranger, had come at an unsocial hour when only close friends were present. But everyone was conscious of the fact that his family was now occupying Yelden Hall.

Dora turned a little pale, but she said at once, 'Not at all. You are very welcome, Mr Grindle. Have you all dined? We were about to go in.'

'No, we have not, but we would not dream of intruding,' said Dudley. 'Besides, we are not dressed for dinner. We were going to eat at our hotel.'

'That I cannot allow,' replied Dora. 'And as for your dress, if we do not regard it, why should you? Do you not agree, Nella?'

Fenella, who had agreed from the first and had only kept silent because after all it was not her house or her table, now lent her voice to the argument. 'Most certainly,' she said. 'Besides, if you go away we shall have no excuse for escaping that wretched concert!'

They all laughed.

'Then if it is a question of obliging you, naturally we shall stay,' said Dudley, smiling. 'Is Charlie to join us?'

Dora coloured only slightly and said calmly enough, 'No, he had another engagement. He will be so sorry to have missed you.' She rang the bell to give instructions for extra places to be laid and a few minutes later, they went in for dinner.

'This is indeed a delightful surprise,' said Dora, once they were all seated at the table. 'When did you decide to come to London? For how long do you intend to stay? Are you fixed here for the season?'

Augusta shook her head. 'Not in any formal sense,' she said. 'Dudley has business in town and I decided to accompany him. Then we discovered that Simon needed to make a visit to London, so we decided to travel together.'

'And how are your family enjoying living in the Cookham area?' Fenella asked Simon, knowing that someone must ask the question.

'Very much,' replied the young man, his voice surprisingly deep and rich in contrast to his somewhat willowy appearance. 'I was brought up in the town, but am beginning to appreciate the country, and once I have come to terms with how noisy it is at night, I'm sure I shall settle there very comfortably.'

'Noisy!' exclaimed Fenella. 'Mr Grindle, you must be jesting, surely! In the country you do not hear the watchman calling the hour, or groups of revellers shouting in the street, or horses' hooves on the cobbles, or dealers setting up their barrows or any of the other thousand and one things that make it impossible to sleep!'

140

'Perhaps not,' agreed Mr Grindle, 'but since we have been in the country, first a fox and a night jar have made their presence felt; then a screech owl has perched outside my window, and given of its best, and on one occasion there was a thunderstorm, my window blew open, and I got soaking wet trying to shut it.'

They all laughed.

'There can be no comparison,' replied Fenella. 'The town is by far the noisier.'

'Maybe,' he replied, smiling, 'but it is a noisiness that I am used to, and we all like the familiar, don't we?'

'In that case, I wonder at your complaining about the rain,' said Fenella demurely. 'It is surely just as wet in the town as it is in the country.'

They all laughed, but Fenella thought that Dora looked a little wistful as she did so, and her heart ached for her sister. How could Charlie have deprived her of the home that she had been so looking forward to occupying?

It was while these thoughts were going through her mind that Simon Grindle approached her and said, in a lowered tone, 'Something has occurred which gives me cause for grave concern. Will you meet me tomorrow in Hyde Park so that I can tell you about it?'

She looked a little startled but she was quick on the uptake and said 'Yes, of course. At what time?'

'At nine o'clock. And come alone.' He

suddenly flushed at the realization of how his words might sound. 'It isn't anything romantic, I promise you,' he assured her.

There was no time for more to be said, as their conversation was interrupted, so between then and the next morning, Fenella wondered several times whether she had heard Simon's words correctly. The following day, however, when she rode into the park, having successfully avoided bringing her groom by means of bribing the stable boy, she saw Simon mounted on a long-tailed grey, riding towards her.

'Good morning,' she said to him cheerfully. 'I have discovered that this is the only time that Hyde Park is really bearable for riding. It is so quiet, one can almost fancy oneself in the country.'

Simon looked at her approvingly. She was fashionably dressed in a rich red riding habit and, as always when on horseback, looked relaxed and in control. 'By Jove, Miss Parrish, I don't think I've ever seen you look so well,' he exclaimed, his eye kindling.

'Don't tell me, after what you said last night, that you really did ask me to come here for the sake of my fine eyes.'

Simon smiled, but behind the smile his expression was serious. 'I wish with all my heart that that was all that it was,' he said, and paused.

'Is it to do with the Hall?' she asked him

tentatively.

He nodded. 'Dudley told me that he had spoken to you when the idea of letting Yelden Hall was first discussed. It is for that reason that I decided to speak to you now.' He paused for a long time, then at length he said, almost as if the words had been dragged out of him, 'Miss Parrish, my father did not tell Dudley the whole. At the very beginning of the business, Lord Yelden told my father that if he liked the Hall, then he would sell it to him.'

Fenella's hands tightened so convulsively on the reins that her horse shied and for a few moments she was absorbed with bringing him back under control. 'Simon, are you sure?' she asked him, forgetting briefly about correct forms, then saying 'I beg your pardon, Mr Grindle. What I meant was, perhaps Charlie was still talking about letting the Hall, or maybe continuing to do so on a more long-term basis, or something.'

'Never mind formality,' he said. 'I don't mind dispensing with it if you don't. I'm afraid it's quite certain. My father consults with me on all business matters these days. Part of the reason I am in London is to authorize the purchase and see the business through.' He paused briefly, then went on, speaking all of a rush. 'Fenella, you can't imagine what torture it was for me last night to eat your sister's bread, knowing what I knew. And she so beautiful and generous in her hospitality, and

143

all unsuspecting of my treachery.'

'*Your* treachery!' exclaimed Fenella. 'Say rather Charlie's treachery! But what is to be done? *Will* your father buy the Hall?'

Catching the hostile note in her voice, Simon said, 'I believe he will. But you must realize that Charlie is determined to sell. If it is not to my father, it'll be to some other person. For Father to refuse Charlie's offer will not result in the Hall's being saved.'

Fenella slumped in the saddle. 'No, you are right,' she agreed. 'I was being unfair. But what on earth am I to say to Dora? Should I tell her? And how?'

There being no immediate answer to any of these questions, they rode on in silence, heading back towards the gates.

After a short time, Fenella asked him, 'Is it known locally yet?' Then she went on quickly, 'But no, of course it cannot be, or I would have heard from Mama and Papa, and goodness knows what they will say. Simon, when I arrived here, Dora did not even know that the Hall had been let!'

He looked very much shocked. 'Did you tell her?' he asked.

'No, but I asked Charlie to do so. He was not very pleased with me. Simon, can you think of any reason why he might want to sell his home?'

He was silent for a moment. 'You are right in thinking that it is not yet known locally. As

144

to the reason, perhaps he has heavy debts to settle, either of his own or his father's. That is the reason why some men have to dispose of their property, I believe.'

She opened her mouth to speak but then closed it again. She had remembered the mortgage on Yelden Hall. Furthermore, she recalled how much changed she felt Charlie had become, and how short tempered he seemed to be at times, even with Dora. She knew little about financial matters, but she knew that he was not the only man who had had to take out a mortgage on his property. Could it be that something more was preying on his mind; something which he could not divulge to anyone?

After a few minutes' thought she said to him, 'Have you been to your father's man of business yet? I mean, is the matter concluded?'

'Not as yet,' he replied. 'I had intended to wait upon him today.'

'Can you put it off for a little while?' pleaded Fenella.

'What do you intend to do?' he asked her curiously.

'I've no idea,' she replied, 'but there must be something. I can't just allow Charlie to dispose of his birthright and that of his unborn child without at least trying to do something to help.'

'I can wait for a short time,' replied Simon.

'But that is all. After all, I am my father's agent and he is depending upon me. Let me know if you think of anything.'

Fenella leaned across and squeezed one of his hands in gratitude. At that moment, she looked up and saw Bev riding towards them.

'Surely that is Mr Beville,' Simon said.

'Yes it is,' Fenella replied.

'But he is very well known in the fashionable world,' he said, in tones which showed how impressed he was. 'Never say that you know him.'

'Well I do,' answered Fenella crossly, then Bev was upon them, and she introduced the two men.

They made stilted conversation for a few moments, and eventually Fenella said, 'If you will excuse us now, Simon must escort me home. My sister will be anxious.'

'She would be even more anxious if she knew about the absence of your groom,' Bev replied. 'No doubt Mr Grindle is unaware of what conduct is proper in the town, but you should not be by now, Miss Parrish. It would be a sad business if your come-out were to be ruined by the slur of impropriety.' Touching his hat, he rode away from them.

Fenella made a sound rather like an infuriated kitten. 'How dare he!' she exclaimed as soon as she was able. 'How dare he lecture me on propriety! When he . . . he . . .' Just in time, she remembered that it would be

146

indelicate to mention his reputation, and his connection with actresses, and she closed her mouth firmly.

'Well perhaps he was right in this instance,' ventured Simon. 'He certainly seems to be at home in London.'

'Well of course he is,' replied Fenella scornfully, forgetting her resolve to be discreet. 'He's known as the Wild Marauder, isn't he?'

'Why is he playing propriety, then?' Simon asked her. It went through her mind that this was not the first time that Bev had taken such a role where she was concerned, but naturally she said nothing about it.

'Oh, I don't know,' she replied shortly.

'Does he perhaps have an interest?' he ventured.

'In me?' she exclaimed, flushing. 'Don't be so absurd.' Her agitation conveyed itself to her horse, who side-stepped nervously, but effortlessly she got it back under control. 'I expect he just wants to be difficult,' she went on, affecting a careless tone. 'Why are we talking about some middle-aged libertine anyway? Tell me about Mama and Papa instead. You haven't said anything about them yet. Is Papa's leg healing well?'

'Progress is slower than he would like,' he answered. 'Of course they are both missing you.' In this easy undemanding manner, they chatted until they got back to the house, but had Fenella been asked to give an account of what had been said, she would have had no more than a vague idea. Most of her mind was given to the appalling tidings which she had received concerning the sale of Yelden Hall. She was very glad to find on their return that Dora had not yet left her room. This meant that she was free to think about what was uppermost in her mind without having to reveal any of it to anyone.

Simon had said, and Bev had implied, that the most likely reason a man would let or sell his home would be because he was short of money, but she hardly needed anyone else to tell her that. The question was, why was he short of money? He was an only child, so there had been no other children to be provided for from the estate. His mother had lived a quiet, retired life, and his father had never seemed to be profligate in his spending. But she was beginning to realize that even those whom she thought she knew well might have secrets in their lives to which their nearest and dearest might not be privy.

It occurred to Fenella that Charlie hardly ever spent an evening at home, and that when he went out, he did not usually go with them, but generally attended a party of his own choosing. Perhaps if she could find out where he went and what he did, she might be able to discover why he needed so much money. Then, once she knew, she could take steps to find a solution to his problem.

CHAPTER TWELVE

'I am so glad that you have come, Augusta,' said Dora, the following morning after breakfast. 'It is like getting a real taste of home.' Augusta and her brother had made arrangements to stay at a hotel, and despite Dora's protests, they would not change their plans. She had begged, however, that Augusta should spend as much time as possible with her. (Simon Grindle was staying with acquaintances of his father, and he had gone there after dinner the previous evening.)

'We have missed you,' Augusta replied.

'And I you,' admitted Dora. 'But I have to confess that I have a rather selfish reason for being so pleased to see you.'

Augusta smiled. 'Let me guess,' she said. 'You would like me to deputize for you and take Fenella about a little.'

'You have read my mind exactly,' replied Dora. 'Of course I am not entirely incapable, and Lady Appleby has been kind enough to offer her services, but—'

Augusta held up her hand. 'I quite understand,' she said. 'You and I have known one another for a long time, haven't we? Of course I will help. I shall be glad to do so.

149

What are today's plans?'

'There are some calls that we must make, but later, after dinner, we may go to Vauxhall Gardens if it stays fine.'

Augusta smiled a little wistfully. 'The last time I went there, I was with Edward,' she said.

'I hope it will not distress you to go,' said Fenella quickly. 'For I would willingly forgo it, rather than that.'

'Not at all,' replied Augusta smiling. 'Thank you for your thoughtfulness, but although our marriage was short, I have nothing but happy memories from it.' Fenella could not help glancing at her sister and wondering whether she could say the same.

Charlie made an appearance during the morning and declared himself delighted to see his old neighbours and playfellows. There appeared to Fenella to be a slight tension between Charlie and Dudley, but it was not sufficient to spoil the atmosphere, and soon Charlie declared his intention of taking Dudley out and introducing him to some of his clubs. This gave Fenella pause for thought. Perhaps, she wondered, it might be possible to find out from Dudley whether Charlie spent any large sums of money in his company? She resolved to question Dudley later.

That day, they called upon Lady Appleby, at Dora's insistence. 'Since we did not attend the concert last night, it is the least we can do,' she insisted. Lady Appleby was delighted to see them, and she had a warm welcome for Augusta whose husband had been a distant relative of hers. Lord Appleby was not at home when they arrived, but he appeared halfway through their call. Fenella's feeling of tepid pleasure at the sight of him confirmed her decision that he was not the man for her, but she was interested to note how animated Augusta became when conversing with him. Perhaps Lord Appleby might prove to be the man who would provide Augusta with her second chance of happiness.

The next call that they made was upon Mrs Maxfield. Mr Maxfield had taken his sister out for a drive, but his wife was not alone for her cousin was with her. This was the first time that Fenella had seen him since their encounter in the park, and she was determined not to seem at all interested in his good opinion. Naturally, this necessitated avoiding his eye, but as she found that this entailed looking at him to see if he was looking at her, it was by no means as easy as it sounded.

Mrs Maxfield was very pleased to meet Augusta, and declared that she remembered her very well from the wedding. She was not as surprised to see them as might have been expected, however.

'Charlie came to see me a little while ago and told me of your visitors,' she told Dora.

'Then we must have just missed him,'

replied Dora. 'We have been calling upon Lady Appleby.'

'And was Lord Appleby at home?' Mrs Maxfield asked, with a roguish look at Fenella. 'All of London has held him to be a confirmed bachelor this age, but now the gossip is of quite another nature. I think that you must plume yourself on your conquest, Miss Parrish.'

'Conquest? I have made no conquest,' Fenella replied hastily, darting a glance at Bev out of the corner of her eye.

'That is not what I have been told,' answered Mrs Maxfield. 'The word is that Lady Appleby will be the Dowager Lady Appleby by this time next year.'

'Then the word lies,' declared Fenella, colouring.

'Well, he who lives longest will see the most,' murmured Mrs Maxfield. 'Tell me, Mrs Brampton, do you intend to make a long stay in London?'

With that, the subject was dropped, but Fenella was left feeling that everyone had received the impression that a match between herself and Lord Appleby was imminent, and her feelings of irritation with Mrs Maxfield increased. She suddenly became aware that apart from Augusta, who had seemed rather taken with the personable baron, there was one other person in the room who must not think anything of the sort!

The next few days proved to be very enjoyable for Fenella. Dora, who had begun to tire quickly, did not always want to go out in the evenings, but Augusta had come to London eager to enjoy herself, and was very ready to take in as many entertainments as Fenella might wish. Their escorts varied from occasion to occasion. Sometimes they were escorted by Dudley and Simon. At other times, Lord Appleby joined them and it soon became obvious that he had transferred his interest to Augusta. Once Fenella had explained to her that, contrary to Mrs Maxfield's belief, she did not aspire to becoming the next Lady Appleby, she seemed ready to make it clear, in the most ladylike way, that the interest was entirely mutual.

Fenella and Dudley drifted into the same easy friendship that they had always enjoyed. The episode in the garden at Yelden Hall, if not completely forgotten, had been discounted as a momentary aberration without any lasting significance. Some members of the polite world, however, seeing the friendship between them, began to think that they might make a match of it. Once Fenella was certain that Dudley had no such aspirations, she was not averse under some circumstances to let the misunderstanding pass. From time to time she would sense Bev's eyes upon her, and then it often seemed necessary for her to talk animatedly with Dudley, or with Simon.

For his part, Dudley seemed to be enjoying London more than might have been expected. He still cast one or two wistful glances at Dora from time to time, but Fenella was pleased to see that he was by no means oblivious to the charms of other ladies. In particular, he seemed rather taken with Miss Maxfield and, although it was difficult to tell with one so shy, she appeared to be similarly interested in him. Fenella wondered whether the quiet, country existence that had been his until recently had not been entirely good for him in that it had made it difficult for him to shake off his romantic attachment to Dora.

Despite the attractions of London life, however, Fenella did not forget the necessity of discovering why Charlie's money had disappeared. She had tried to find out information from Dudley but he had proved to be disappointingly reticent.

'It would be quite improper for me to tell you about what takes place at a gentleman's club,' he told her.

'Bother what's proper,' she replied, stamping her foot. 'I suppose what you mean is that it would be against some stupid male code of honour.'

'Yes, it would,' he replied. 'I cannot possibly tell you what goes on. It would be like breaking an oath, or betraying a confidence.'

Fenella opened her mouth to protest, but then closed it again. Annoying though she

154

found Dudley's adherence to this male code, she had to respect it, however reluctantly. It was after all through a sense of loyalty to Charlie and Dora that she was keeping quiet about her concerns and suspicions. In any case, she could not speak about the selling of the Hall since Simon had bound her to secrecy.

Fenella tried to make sure that she dined at home frequently so that Dora would not feel neglected. Dudley and Augusta often joined them, together with Simon Grindle, but Charlie was seldom of their number. Even though he knew that his wife could go out very little now, he rarely curtailed his amusements for her sake.

Fenella found herself wondering more and more whether Charlie had gambled his money away. The more she was in town, the more she realized that everyone gambled, and some did so to excess. She had played a little herself at silver loo one evening, and had been horrified to discover how much it was possible to lose in a very short space of time. The code appeared to be that however much one lost, one demonstrated an attitude of unconcern towards one's losses and never showed the slightest doubt of one's ability to pay. The trouble was, that since Charlie so rarely attended the same evening functions as his wife, it was proving to be almost impossible to observe his habits.

One evening, however, Fenella gained some insight into the way that Charlie spent his time; it was not to be an insight that cheered her in any way.

They had attended a small soirée in Mount Street, and since Dora had become a little tired, Simon escorted the two sisters home early. It was only a short journey from Mount Street to Curzon Street, but it proved to be eventful in its way. They were just turning into South Audley Street, when they heard rowdy male voices.

'Don't look outside,' said Dora quickly. 'Probably some gentlemen are drunk, and it is far better for us not to seem to notice them at all.' Dora was facing the horses, and she instantly looked away from the source of the noise, and Simon, noting her unease, engaged her in conversation. Fenella, however, rather in the manner of one instructed not to go near the edge of a cliff, or touch something hot, instantly found herself unable to resist looking out of the window as they passed. By the light of the flambeaux outside a house, she saw a group of gentlemen noisily making merry. Most of them were unknown to her, but, as she was watching, one of them turned towards the carriage, and she saw that it was Charlie. She opened her mouth to say so, then realized that Dora would scarcely thank her for drawing her attention to her husband when he was in this condition.

As she watched, another man turned, laughing, to clap Charlie on the shoulder, and she realized that it was Bev. Well, Fenella told herself, you knew that he was the Wild Marauder. What did you expect? The truth was that she did not think that she would see Bev egging Charlie on to behave in such a manner, especially when she had revealed to him something of her concern for her brother-in-law; and the knowledge that he had done so made her feel disappointed. Then the carriage travelled on, and the moment passed.

*   *   *

'Time to go home, Charlie,' said Bev. He had been walking home from an evening of piquet with Lord Richard Byles when he had encountered Charlie and his friends on the street corner. Moments after his arrival, the Yelden carriage had gone by and although he had not seen the ladies inside, he had recognized Charlie's carriage and knew that Dora and Fenella must be on their way home.

'Home? Now?' exclaimed one of the other men. 'Are you mad, Bev?'

'Yes, he's mad,' declared one of the others, and they all started to laugh.

'The night's young yet,' declared Charlie, swaying. 'Who's for a hand of cards at Haverson's? How about you, Bev?'

Bev shook his head. 'I've gambled my fill

this evening,' he declared. 'And you shouldn't be gambling in your condition. Dammit, man, you won't even be able to see the cards.'

'Course he will,' hiccoughed one of the other men. 'Come on, Charlie. Are you in, or not?'

'I'm in,' replied Charlie. 'Go home, Bev—to your slippers and warming pan!'

With a roar of laughter, the group proceeded on their way. Bev stared after them for a moment or two. It seemed a very long time since he, too, had been one of such a group. It had been in such a manner that he had earned his reputation and his nickname. Perhaps he *was* only fit for his slippers and warming pan, he mused ironically. He enjoyed all kinds of social pursuits as much as the next man; but such behaviour as Charlie's could easily lead to his ruin. Of course, he might be making too much of it, but there had been that in Charlie's avid expression when he had seen him in the gaming hell, which had seemed to suggest that gaming and drunkenness were now a way of life for him, rather than a momentary aberration. And any disgrace that touched him would affect his wife and unborn child, and probably his sister-in-law as well.

Shaking off his momentary abstraction, he walked on to his lodgings.

CHAPTER THIRTEEN

Just as Fenella was beginning to think that she would have to admit defeat over the question of observing Charlie, her chance to do so came quite unexpectedly. On one of the rare occasions when he was dining at home, one of his friends who had joined them there had to leave early. Fenella chanced to be about to descend the stairs when Charlie was seeing his friend to the door.

'Tomorrow at Ranelagh,' he said, as the man was leaving. 'I've come into a bit of capital and I mean to make you smart for your victory yesterday.'

'I'm your man,' said the other. 'At ten o'clock?'

'By all means. I'll tell the others.'

Fenella waited until Charlie had returned to the drawing-room before making her descent. Ranelagh! She had not been to the famous pleasure gardens, but she knew that people went there to dance, flirt, eat, and also to gamble. She was determined to go, to discover whether what she suspected about Charlie was true. Then if her suspicions were correct, she would have to decide whether to tell Dora what she had found out, or to confront Charlie herself. She shivered at the thought. When she had challenged him about letting the Hall, she

159

had seen a side of him that she had never seen before and that made her a little afraid. Perhaps telling Dora might be the best course of action in any case. Surely he would listen to his own wife? Fenella was certain that deep down he still loved her, but the excitement of town life had made him neglectful.

The need to observe Charlie was clear, but the question was, how to do it? To manufacture an excuse not to go to Lady Beckwith's ball the following night would be simple; she had but to say that she had a headache. The question was, how to get to Ranelagh once the excuse had been made? In the country, she was accustomed to moving about quite freely. She had not been in London for as much as a day, however, before she realized that she would not have the same freedom in town.

What she needed was a fellow conspirator; but who to ask? Dudley had already expressed his unwillingness to enlighten her with regard to Charlie's unfortunate tendency. He was also just close enough to being an elder brother to put obstacles in the way of her outing to Ranelagh, even if she invented another reason for going.

She thought of asking Bev, for of all her acquaintance, he seemed to be the one who would be most at home in such a place, but she was conscious of a strange reluctance to do so. For one thing, she could not shake off the distaste that she had felt when she had seen him carousing in the street with Charlie. For another, she recalled how on another occasion he had kissed her in order to warn her not to be careless of her reputation. What might he think himself entitled to do if she asked him to accompany her on a clandestine visit to Ranelagh? When this thought gave rise to another, namely that it might be worth asking him just to satisfy her curiosity, she sternly repressed it. This was certainly not thinking as a well-bred girl should!

A night's cogitation yielded no answers, and the following morning she was still trying to decide what to do. The only possibility that occurred to her was that she might admit Millie into her confidence and entrust her with the task of summoning a sedan chair, but this course of action was not without its risks. First of all, Millie had been in the employ of the Parrish family all her life, and she might feel it incumbent upon her to inform Dora that her younger sister was doing something so risky. Secondly, there were reliable chairmen, and there were rogues, and Millie, being only a country girl, might not be able to tell the difference. Thirdly, even with Millie's company, to attend Ranelagh without a male escort would be a perilous business. Fenella sighed with frustration.

She was pacing the drawing-room still trying to think of a solution to her dilemma when the butler entered and announced Simon Grindle. It so happened that Dora was speaking with the housekeeper, so Fenella was alone, and in the young man who had just arrived, she suddenly saw the answer to her problem. Of course, the butler, very properly, left the door open, but that did not prevent Fenella from beckoning Mr Grindle over to the window so that they might converse unheard.

'Simon, my sister will return at any moment, so I must ask you directly without any preamble; are you free tonight, and will you accompany me on an errand of . . . of discovery?'

Mr Grindle's eyes brightened. He was still young enough to relish an adventure. 'I should say,' he replied at once. 'Tell me when and where, and I'm your man!'

Fenella could hear her sister's footsteps in the hall and she only just had time to say, 'Bring a sedan chair to the back gate at ten o'clock and wait for me there.'

When Dora entered the room, she could hear her sister brightly pointing out some of the buildings that could be seen from the window.

Thinking of the role that she would have to play, Fenella allowed herself to become increasingly subdued as the day wore on so that when the time came to prepare for the ball, Dora was not at all surprised when her sister pleaded a headache.

162

'I thought that you seemed a little quiet,' she said. 'Such a pity, though, because I thought that I might go tonight, but as you are not well . . .'

'No!' exclaimed Fenella. Then realizing that her tone had been a little too vigorous for one suffering from a headache, she said again in a quieter tone, 'No, Dora. I should never be able to rest, knowing that I had spoiled your pleasure, especially since you go out so seldom now. Millie will look after me very well and so you may be easy.'

At first unsure, Dora allowed herself to be persuaded, and when eventually she and Augusta had both wished the sufferer a fond and sympathetic farewell, Fenella was free to make her own preparations.

It proved impossible not to take Millie into her confidence with regard to her destination that night, although she was very careful not to do so until Dora was safely on her way. At first, the girl was reluctant to give assistance for an enterprise that was clearly clandestine. In the end, since Fenella could not possibly betray Charlie so far as to reveal that she was spying upon him, she was forced to pretend that she was meeting someone.

'Who might it be, Miss Fenella?' Millie asked, as she got her ready, her established status giving her the confidence to ask such a question.

'Oh . . . er . . . Mr Beville,' said Fenella

quickly. Quite why she did not say 'Mr Grindle' she could not have explained, but having given one gentleman's name, she could not possibly arouse suspicion by changing the name of the gentleman whom she was meeting.

'Ooh, Miss Fenella!' exclaimed Millie. 'He's ever so handsome, isn't he?'

Fenella was on the point of saying that she hadn't noticed and didn't care either, but it occurred to her just in time that this might be rather a strange response from a woman who was interested enough in a man to meet him clandestinely, so she simply said, 'Yes.'

'And so elegant too—very well dressed, he is.'

'Yes,' agreed Fenella again.

'What beats me though, miss, is why you have to meet him secretly. Is it because he's called the Wild Marauder?'

'Yes,' said Fenella for the third time.

'Well, I suppose I can understand that, but it does seem a pity.'

Soon, it was time for Fenella to go downstairs to meet Simon. It took her some little while to persuade Millie that it would not be a good idea for her to accompany her mistress.

'I shall need you to wait downstairs and let me in through the back door,' she told her. 'Don't worry, I shall be back home long before the others.'

Millie looked less than happy at this arrangement, but she could see the sense of it. 'Make sure you are, Miss Fenella,' she said. 'If they get back first and think to question me, I shan't know what to say and I can't lie to save my life; you know I can't.'

'Don't worry,' said Fenella again. 'I shan't be long.' When at last she had finished reassuring Millie, she was ten minutes late to meet Simon who was waiting by the sedan chair which he had procured, according to her instructions.

'When you didn't come at ten, I wondered whether I had mistaken what you said,' he told her. 'What instructions would you like me to give to the chairmen?'

'To Ranelagh, if you please,' she said.

'You heard the lady,' declared Simon cheerfully. 'To Ranelagh!'

It took much longer to get to Ranelagh than Fenella had expected. It was a fine evening and despite the fact that it was rather cool, a good many people had clearly been tempted to sample the delights that the famous gardens could offer.

The next problem occurred when they arrived and Fenella saw the extent of the place. In thinking about the evening's errand, she had taken into account neither the size of Ranelagh nor the number of persons who would be present. How would she ever find Charlie in such a crowd?

'Now what?' said Simon. 'Shall we have some supper, or would you like to dance?'

Fenella looked at him in consternation. She had given no thought to what Simon would expect to do once they were at Ranelagh, or indeed how she might contrive to get rid of him in order to set her plans in motion. If he remained with her, it would be impossible for her to do what she had intended to do without confiding in him, but how could she do that? It was true that Simon did know a certain amount about their affairs because of the possible sale of Yelden Hall, but she shrank from the family disloyalty involved in divulging her suspicions. And Simon himself would similarly be bound by family loyalty to his father, and might feel that to know any more about Charlie's affairs would be to compromise that loyalty. But if she merely said that she wanted to see Charlie, he would surely find it very strange for her to be seeking out a man in whose house she was residing.

Just as she found herself unable to give the real reason for her presence there, however, she also found it impossible to tell him the same lie that she had told Millie. Simon was an intelligent young man, and he would certainly not believe that she was meeting Bev, for one very good reason: if that were the case, then why had Bev not been the one to meet her with the sedan chair?

The only thing for it would be to give the

166

impression that she had simply wanted to come to Ranelagh for the adventure. That being the case, she agreed brightly that they could have some supper and perhaps dance a little later. Truth to tell, she was rather hungry, since to lend verisimilitude to the lie that she was not well, she had not done justice to her dinner. Perhaps now that they were there an idea would come to her. After all, she reflected, the opportunity to come to Ranelagh had been providential. Perhaps luck would favour her again.

As time passed, however, she began to wonder whether her errand might be fruitless after all. They had supper together and danced several dances, all of which in other circumstances Fenella would have very much enjoyed, for Simon was a good dancer, and made very lively company. Then, when they were leaving the floor after a country dance, Simon said, 'Do you see that man over there in the green coat? I could swear that that is Bruce Bentley, who was with me at Oxford.' Fenella looked where he was pointing, and at that moment the man in the green coat turned slightly. 'By Jove it is,' he went on. 'Forgive me, Fenella, if I go and speak to him, will you? I won't be more than a minute or two.' She sat down to wait for him, and amused herself by taking in all the details of the apparel and behaviour of those around her. Some were masked, like herself. Others clearly did not mind who recognized them in such a place.

Then, as she was watching the crowd, she suddenly had a sensation of being observed herself, and turning her head, she saw Bev standing still and looking in her direction. As always, he looked more elegant than any of those around him. He was unmasked, and dressed on this occasion in his black evening dress with the red shot-silk waistcoat. With his dark hair unpowdered, he stood out from any other man present.

For one dreadful moment, she thought that he had recognized her and was about to approach her. Then, from behind where she was standing, she heard a rustle of skirts, and past her swayed the actress whom she had seen at the inn at Hounslow, and again at Drury Lane. Together with another woman, she crossed the rotunda, and greeted Bev with a smile. Fenella turned away crossly, failing to see Bev darting another keen glance in her direction.

Moments later, Simon returned to her side. 'I'm glad I saw Bentley,' he said. 'He was quite a decent fellow and I'd not spoken to him for ages. Do you want to dance again, or shall we have a stroll around?'

'Let's walk about a little,' Fenella replied, shaking off the feeling of depression which had suddenly come upon her. If they saw more of the pleasure gardens, she decided, they might catch sight of Charlie and his party.

It was when she had almost despaired of succeeding in her mission that she had the most amazing luck. Looking round at the crowd, she spotted the man with whom Charlie had made the rendezvous the previous night.

'Oh!' she exclaimed.

'What is it?' Simon asked her.

'Just over there,' Fenella said, improvising rapidly. 'That university friend of yours, Mr Bentley, is over there, beckoning to you.'

'Where?' Simon asked, showing no inclination to move.

'Over there,' Fenella said anxiously. She did not want to lose sight of Charlie's friend.

Simon looked towards where she was pointing. 'I can't see him,' he said. 'Anyway, I've spoken to him now.'

'But I think he really wants to speak to you,' insisted Fenella. 'He's looking very anxious.'

'You must have very good eyes, because I can't see him at all,' said Simon, craning his neck. 'If he wants to see me, why the deuce doesn't he come over here?'

'I don't know,' replied Fenella, only refraining from stamping her foot with great difficulty. 'Perhaps he can't. Perhaps he's . . . he's stuck in something, or . . . or . . .'

'*Stuck* in something?' Simon exclaimed incredulously. 'What on earth do you mean?'

'Oh I don't know,' Fenella exclaimed, her exasperation almost getting the better of her. 'But he might have hurt himself or . . . Oh

Simon, please go and see him before it's too late!'

'Well, what about you?' he asked her. 'I can't just leave you.'

'Go and see him,' she urged. Charlie's friend was almost out of sight now. 'I'll be quite safe here. Hurry!'

Simon looked at her suspiciously, opened his mouth, closed it again, and walked over to where she was pointing. As soon as his back was turned, Fenella hurried after her quarry. Fortunately, he was wearing a very distinctive salmon pink coat, so he was easy to observe. At one stage, she feared that in her anxiety not to lose sight of him again she had drawn too close, for the man halted, stiffened and appeared about to turn round. He did not do so however, and with a sigh, she fell back a little and followed him at a greater distance.

At length, he came to one of the booths set outside the rotunda for the use of gentlemen who wished to smoke. A general hubbub of welcome greeted the newcomer as he entered. Then the curtains at the entrance were closed behind him. Stifling a little cry of frustration, Fenella crept round to the side of the booth and found, to her satisfaction, a small window. The curtains were drawn across it, but this had been carelessly done and she found that by standing on tiptoe she was able to set her eye to the gap and observe what was going on.

There were five men present apart from the

new arrival. One of them was Charlie and, which almost made her gasp with surprise, Bev was another. The table was covered with cards, money and notes of hand, and the number of glasses and bottles bore witness to the kind of evening that it had been. Charlie's face was flushed and his wig was askew. It seemed to Fenella that there was very little money left at his elbow.

'Luck against you, Yelden?' asked the newcomer.

'Only tonight so far,' replied Charlie. 'But don't worry; I shall come about. I have a new system which is bound to work. Besides, I've got money coming in soon. Come along, let's deal again. Are you in, Crofts?'

'By your leave,' replied Crofts sitting down.

Bev was sitting next to Charlie, facing the window and, although it was surely impossible, it seemed for a moment to Fenella as if he was looking straight at her. She watched the play for a short time. She could not understand the game at all, but it seemed to her that whatever Charlie's system might be it was not as yet working in his favour. The small pile of money at his elbow soon disappeared, and then he began signing pieces of paper and laying them out in place of money. The pile at Bev's elbow was growing all the time. Suddenly she felt angry that Bev should thus profit from another man's weakness, quite forgetting that there were other men present, who also had money to hand.

At that moment, her observations were interrupted by a voice from behind her saying, 'What are you about, wench? Are you spying, egad?'

At first unconcerned with anything save the need to remain undiscovered, she turned round, placing her finger to her lips, and said 'Sshh!'

The stout, red-faced man standing behind her set his hands on his hips. 'Undoubtedly a spy,' he declared in the same carrying tones. 'Hey there! You inside! There's a spy observing you!' He stepped forward and seized hold of her arm in a firm grip. 'Let's see your face, wench,' he said, making as if to remove her mask. She stared at him in consternation, but before he could make good his words, Bev emerged from the booth.

'Release the girl,' he said amiably. 'I know who she is, and she's spying on me for a wager, I'll be bound.'

'Beville, ain't it?' said the stout man. 'Give you good evening. You know her, you say?'

'Indeed I do,' replied Bev, 'And I'll deal with her in my own way.'

'Then I wish you joy of her,' said the other man, laughing as he walked away.

'Come, miss,' said Bev, taking hold of Fenella by the arm which the stout man had only just released. 'Let's get you away from here before the others come out.'

'I fear I do not know you, sir,' said Fenella trying to disguise her voice.

'Don't be so damn' silly,' he replied, walking away from the booth and retaining hold of her arm so that she was forced to walk with him, half-running because he was setting a brisk pace. 'I saw you earlier across the rotunda and recognized you at once. Tell me, Miss Parrish, what idiot did you inveigle into bringing you here tonight?'

Instead of answering his question, she responded with one of her own. 'Will you *please* slow down?' she exclaimed, half panting.

He did so, then stopped, saying, 'I don't suppose any of the party will pursue us now.'

'How do you know that I am not here with a party of my own?' she asked him, tossing her head. Then as he opened his mouth again, she went on quickly, 'And don't tell me not to be so . . . so damn' silly again, because I am not.'

He looked down at her, her face flushed, her bosom heaving, and he felt his heart miss a beat, but because he was unexpectedly touched and did not know what to do, he laughed. 'It is quite plain that you are not here with a party,' he replied. 'Your sister and her friends are at Lady Beckwith's tonight and Charlie is here with an exclusively male group. With what other party could you have come?' She looked away. He sighed. 'With you I seem constantly to have to preach propriety and it's a very unfamiliar role. Yet here am I having

173

to do so again. You really shouldn't be here alone, you know.'

'I didn't come alone,' she said swiftly.

'And who brought you?' he asked her softly. She was silent. 'I see. May I ask you who this gentleman might be, or where he is?'

'How do you know it was a gentleman?' she asked him challengingly. 'In any case, it's none of your business. I haven't been asking you the name of the lightskirt you were with, have I?'

'And what do you know of lightskirts, miss?' he asked her.

'Not as much as you, obviously,' she replied, tossing her head.

At that, his temper snapped. 'For God's sake, Fenella,' he said exasperatedly. 'Stop playing games with me. You are here, in a place where no woman should be alone, unless she's of easy virtue. You've clearly inveigled some poor fool into giving you his escort and now you've given him the slip. Heaven alone knows what he thinks has happened to you. As if all that were not enough, I have discovered you engaged in an activity of a reprehensible nature, namely spying on gentlemen through a half-closed curtain. It's now one o'clock in the morning. How do you expect to get home, and how will you explain your absence?'

She paled, for out of his whole speech, one item of information had leaped to her notice. 'One o'clock! It cannot be!'

'Indeed it is,' he replied and, as if to mock

174

her, a distant clock chimed the hour.

'I must go home at once! I must not be missed!' she exclaimed, her voice betraying more than a touch of anxiety. She turned to flee, then realized that she did not know which way to go.

'I'll take you,' said Bev with a sigh. 'Come with me.' She hesitated. 'You're perfectly safe,' he assured her. 'Or is that what concerns you? Would you have liked this adventure to have been spiced with a little more danger?' He pulled her into his arms and looked down into her troubled face. Then with a light laugh, he dropped a kiss on her brow. 'Come, you absurd child,' he said, in a gentler tone than he had used so far that night, 'let's get you home before they send out the militia.'

Although the streets were still busy outside, it seemed to be only the work of a moment for Bev to procure a sedan chair, and soon they were setting a brisk pace back to Curzon Street.

As they drew near, Fenella attracted Bev's attention and said, 'We must go to the back door. Millie will be up, waiting for me.'

Bev observed the blaze of light coming from the Yelden residence and silently decided that there were almost certainly more people waiting for them than Millie, but he said nothing and simply directed the chair men to the back entrance. He helped Fenella out and paid off the men.

She held her hand out to him, saying, rather stiffly because she had not forgotten his words of criticism, 'Thank you, sir, for bringing me home.'

He bowed over her hand, but did not release it. 'I will see you to the door,' he said, 'just in case some mischance has occurred and Millie is not there to let you in.'

They crossed the small town garden and Millie opened the door, but she looked very frightened. 'Oh miss, I'm so very sorry,' she stammered. 'But my lady came home early and looked in on you and you weren't there so she sent for me and . . . and . . . I just had to tell her, Miss Fenella!'

'You told her?' whispered Fenella. 'What exactly did you tell her?'

'Everything, miss!' replied Millie, who then burst into tears.

CHAPTER FOURTEEN

'Come on, let's go in,' said Bev.

Fenella looked at him in consternation. 'You are not coming in as well, surely?' she said to him. 'We *shall* be in the suds then.'

'What do you propose I do instead?' he asked her. 'Run away, leaving you to face the fire alone?'

'But there is no need,' she protested. 'My

176

sister has no reason to connect you with my . . . my escapade. She does not know that you . . .' Her eye caught Millie's and she stopped abruptly. 'You even told her that, didn't you?'

Millie, whose sobs had subsided into sniffles, began to cry again, twisting the corner of her apron into a screw. 'Miss Fenella, I told you I couldn't lie, and you did say that you was meeting Mr Beville.'

'Oh did she?' said Bev, his eye gleaming. 'Then in that case, it is clearly incumbent upon me to make an appearance. Come, my dear.' He held out his arm to Fenella, and she looked up at him as she took it. Suddenly she realized that by accompanying her like this, he was walking into a trap, and furthermore that he probably knew it better than she. Despite this, however, he did not look at all concerned. She wondered whether perhaps he had thought of a way out of the mess.

They entered the drawing-room to find Dora present, and with her Simon Grindle. When he saw her, he started forward. 'Fenella! I mean, Miss Parrish! Whatever happened? I was only gone for a short time, but when I came back, you had vanished!'

'That answers one of my questions,' murmured Mr Beville, in a tone so low that only Fenella could hear him.

'Simon, I'm sorry, I—' Fenella began, but she did not have a chance to finish.

'Fenella!' exclaimed Dora. Fenella had

never seen her sister so angry, and the use of her name in full betrayed just how angry she was. 'What is the meaning of this? I returned from the Beckwiths' and came to see how you were, only to discover that your bed was empty and had not been slept in. Millie told me that you had gone to Ranelagh with Mr Beville, but then Mr Grindle arrived, saying that *he* had taken you to Ranelagh. Now, you appear with Mr Beville! Upon my word, Fenella, I do not know what to think! With which of these two gentlemen did you go, and with whom did you spend your time whilst you were there?'

'Dora, I am so very sorry,' said Fenella in a mortified tone.

'I should think you are! To think that I had been so looking forward to your coming to London! Upon my soul, I have a good mind to send both you and Millie back to Mama in disgrace!'

'Dora, please don't do that!' exclaimed Fenella, horrified.

'I do not see that I have any alternative,' said Dora, the very picture of the outraged matron. 'And as for you—Mr Beville, and Mr Grindle—I do not know which of the two of you has behaved more shamefully!'

'Lady Yelden,' began Simon, colouring with mortification.

Before he could say any more, however, Bev held up his hand. 'There is no question of that, Lady Yelden,' he said, with a great air of

178

frankness. 'I have undoubtedly behaved the more reprehensibly. It is true that Mr Grindle brought your sister to Ranelagh, but it was only at my behest, since I had another engagement which I was obliged to fulfil first. I was the one she met there, and I acknowledge that I did wrong in persuading an innocent young girl into clandestine activity.' He took hold of Fenella's hand once more and tucked it in his arm. 'I pledge you my word that my future dealings with her will be completely honourable and, if you will give me leave, I will make it my life's study to protect the honour of her name.'

For a few moments, there was complete silence in the room. Then Dora said in a much calmer voice, 'Mr Beville, if you wanted to court my sister, why could you not do so in a more honourable way? You have never been forbidden this house. It hurts me that you should behave in this manner towards my family when there was no need of it.'

Bev looked down at Fenella, then looked across at Dora again. 'You cannot reproach me more than I reproach myself,' he said seriously. 'The truth is that I allowed the romance of the situation to carry me along and lure me into wrong doing.'

Fenella had stood listening to the conversation so far, a prey to so many different emotions that she was only taking in half of what was being said. When Dora had spoken to her in such an angry way, she had felt a mixture of shock and fear. This had surprised her, for of the two of them, she, Fenella, had always been the more dominant one. Then she had felt ashamed that she should have caused her sister such anxiety in her present condition. She was horrified when her sister had turned on Simon and Bev, and then astonished when Bev had taken the blame for the whole evening. It occurred to her that of the three of them—herself, Simon and Bev— Bev was the only one who was guiltless in this matter. All he had done was act to protect her from exposure and bring her home safely, and yet he was taking all the blame.

She took a step forward and said, 'No! No, it is not true. Mr Beville is not to blame, and nor is Simon. It is all my fault!'

Dora permitted her face to soften into a smile. 'Nella, you're always so impulsive! I cannot condone what has happened, but at least it appears that there is to be a happy ending. Mr Beville, I believe it would be best for you to go and see my father tomorrow. For now, we shall bid you goodnight.'

Bev made a magnificent bow. 'Thank you for your forbearance, my lady,' he said. Then, turning to Fenella, he lifted her hand to his lips and kissed it lingeringly. '*A bientôt*,' he said, turning to leave.

Simon bowed formally. 'Once more, I offer you my sincere apologies, my lady,' he said.

180

'Believe me, I would rather do anything on earth than distress you.'

Dora inclined her head graciously, then the two men left.

'Dora, I don't understand,' Fenella said after they had gone. 'Why is Bev . . . I mean, Mr Beville, to go and see Papa?'

Dora smiled. 'Nella, my dear, don't you understand? You are to be engaged to him.'

*   *   *

After they had left the house, Bev and Simon walked along in silence for a short time. Eventually, Bev said, 'Tell me, whose idea was it that you should go to Ranelagh tonight?'

'Well . . . it was mine, of course,' replied Simon defensively after a moment's hesitation.

'Was it a romantic assignation?' Bev asked him. 'After all, I should hate to be treading on your toes.'

'Good heavens, no,' exclaimed Simon. 'Nothing of the sort!' It suddenly occurred to him that such a reply, although it might reassure Bev that he had no claims upon his betrothed, sounded less than gallant, so he added, 'She's a splendid girl, but not . . . not for me, you know.'

'Just so,' agreed Bev. 'By the way, did she tell you why she wanted to go, or did she just lead you by the nose?'

'No, she didn't tell me, I just assumed—' He

stopped abruptly. 'You knew that it was her idea then,' he said in a relieved tone.

'I guessed,' replied Bev.

'So she wasn't going to meet you?'

Bev shook his head. 'Our meeting there was pure coincidence,' he said. 'If you dare to repeat that, however, I shall skin you alive.'

After a few moments' thought, Simon said, 'When she first suggested that we go, I thought that perhaps it was just for a lark. But now I think about it, there was a kind of . . . well, I suppose you could call it watchfulness, about her. She managed to shake me off with such a ridiculous tale that I wonder now why I fell for it.' He paused in thought for a moment. 'The one thing I cannot forgive myself for is causing Lady Yelden such distress. I must go back and apologize as soon as possible.'

Bev did not reply, and in a very short time, they had reached the house where Simon was staying. Before the two men parted, he turned and said to Bev, 'Do you know, it has just occurred to me that since you were not meeting Fenella there, then it should be I who should . . . should . . .'

Bev grinned at him, his teeth gleaming by the light of the flambeaux. 'So it should,' he said. 'Some men have all the luck, don't they?'

*   *   *

It was a long time before Fenella managed to

get to sleep that night. Her original mission had been accomplished. She had arrived at the booth well after eleven o'clock, to discover that Charlie was still gambling, and every indication was that he had been losing heavily for some time. Although this discovery gave her no satisfaction, and indeed caused her considerable worry, at least it meant that she could now try to decide what to do. Her inclination was still to approach Dora with her knowledge. It would be necessary to pick the moment, but it was surely wrong that her sister should remain in ignorance of the way in which her husband was dissipating their fortune.

Although she had succeeded in her objective, however, other things had happened which threatened to dominate her thoughts. Reluctantly, she had to admit that her discovery by Bev and his escorting her home were causes for thankfulness. Had he not appeared, there was no telling how she would have got back to Curzon Street, for she would never have found Simon again, and she had no idea how to summon a sedan chair for herself. On the other hand, his interference had meant that Dora had seen them together and made all kind of assumptions, and because of those assumptions, he had been forced to protect her name by offering marriage.

She told herself that that was not at all what she wanted. For one thing, she had seen him meeting an actress that very evening. For another, and just as disturbingly, she had seen him in a card game profiting from Charlie's weakness. There was undoubtedly ample reason for her to disentangle herself as quickly as possible from her engagement to one who was clearly profligate and a womanizer. The problem was, she was forced to admit, that if his failings could somehow be explained away, and if only he had not been forced into making her an offer, to marry him would suit her very well indeed.

*　　*　　*

The following day, Fenella was expecting to face a barrage of criticism from her sister for the previous night's escapade, but beyond a pointed comment about its being such a good thing that Bev was a gentleman, she showed no inclination to discuss the matter further.

In order to test the seriousness of the situation, Fenella said, 'Is it really important that Bev and I should become engaged? After all, no one else knew about it but yourself and Simon.'

'My dear, it is vital,' Dora assured her. '*You* may not think that anyone else saw you, but you may be sure that in such circumstances *someone* would see you—it always happens! A young girl cannot be too careful of her reputation. The merest hint of a scandal would be enough to ruin all your chances.' She paused for a moment as if weighing her words. 'You must forgive me for saying this, but the fact that you were with Bev would particularly count against you, because of his reputation.'

'As the Wild Marauder?' suggested Fenella.

Dora nodded. 'I imagine that the name was probably earned in his youth and is now something that he regrets,' she said. 'But nevertheless, people are slow to forget that kind of thing.'

'Women are very attracted to him,' Fenella said slowly.

'Yes they are, and I think I know why,' replied her sister, after a moment's consideration. 'Of course he is handsome and charming, but I think that the real reason for his popularity is because when you are talking to him, he gives you his whole attention—as if nothing else in the world mattered except what you have to say.'

Fenella nodded thoughtfully, but no more was said on this matter, and soon Dora was talking of bride clothes.

Later when she went back to her room during the morning, Fenella thought again about her engagement. She had a very strong sense of justice, and it still seemed unfair to her that Bev should have taken the blame when he was in no way in the wrong. An engagement that had been wrung from a gentleman out of duty was surely doomed to

185

failure. Perhaps, she wondered, it might be broken off later with the excuse that they were not suited. It was a strangely depressing thought.

Hardly less depressing was the conviction that now that she knew of Charlie's weakness, she must do something about it. Part of her believed that she should challenge him with what she knew, and yet she felt very unsure of herself in this respect. It would have been good to ask Bev's advice, but Bev had gone to see her father, and in any case, after she had seen him win money from Charlie, she was not entirely sure how far she could trust him.

There was another reason why she did not want to challenge Charlie at present. It had not escaped her attention that there was an increased degree of tension between Lord and Lady Yelden. It could be seen in Charlie's grudging accompanying of his wife to social occasions, and in the anxious expression which Dora wore more often than her sister liked. Fenella had no wish to make bad worse.

In the event, Charlie showed such delight at the news of the engagement that a happy atmosphere was restored. He came into the drawing-room in high good humour, bearing with him Dora's pearls which, he said, had been cleaned, and the clasp made more secure.

Dora professed herself very glad to have them back. 'I shall be able to wear them for the engagement party,' she said happily. She had told him nothing about the scene after Fenella's return from Ranelagh, letting him believe that it was merely a somewhat hasty but perfectly natural decision, untainted by any impropriety.

'You'll have some agreeable relatives in Connie and her husband,' he said to Fenella.

'Yes of course,' she agreed. It had not occurred to her that she would be related to Mrs Maxfield and she found herself thinking that she was not so delighted about it as Charlie appeared to be.

'It will be a great advantage for you to have such a friend in town,' he went on.

'But I shall have Dora after all,' replied Fenella.

'Yes but I shall not be here for so long now,' said Dora. 'I shall want to go down to Yelden Hall with baby as soon as it can be arranged. Have you told the Grindles that we shall want the Hall back in the summer?' she asked Charlie.

He stared at her. 'We have agreed no such thing,' he said evenly, his face unsmiling.

At that unfortunate moment, Simon Grindle was announced, and he declared that he had come to wish Fenella joy on her engagement.

'How did you know about it?' Charlie asked him suspiciously.

'Had it off Bev,' Simon replied

imperturbably. 'I saw him before he set off for Brightstones. Haven't got you a present yet,' he went on, turning to Fenella. 'Or does one not give presents on an engagement?'

Dora laughed. 'For my part, I think that any occasion is a good excuse for giving a present. Mr Grindle, are your parents enjoying living at Yelden Hall?'

He looked watchful. 'Certainly they are,' he replied, after only a brief pause. 'They like the area very much.'

'Do you think that they will be able to vacate for the summer?' Dora went on, regardless of Charlie's lowering expression. 'I should very much like to take the new Viscount Burchett there after he is born.'

Simon looked at Dora's happy face and at Charlie's angry one, and merely said that he had no idea of their intentions.

'In any case,' Charlie put in, 'I have it in mind to take you to the seaside this summer—perhaps to Lyme Regis. Dr Driver thinks very highly of Lyme.'

'Well, we shall see,' answered Dora, looking unconvinced. She was very well aware, however, that to have an argument about their arrangements in front of Simon would be bad manners, so she changed the subject, saying, 'Oh Mr Grindle, do look at my pearls! Charlie had them cleaned and he has collected them from the jeweller today. Are they not fine?' She held the box out for his inspection.

He looked at them in the box for a long moment, then took out his quizzing glass, said, 'May I?' and picked them up to examine them more closely.

Afterwards, he could not have explained his indiscretion, except possibly to say that having been the model of tact over the subject of Yelden Hall, he had now allowed his guard to slip. 'I'm afraid you will have to have words with your jeweller, my lord,' he said eventually, his tone grave. 'These pearls are forgeries.'

Dora gasped and staggered back a little and Fenella turned white, remembering what Charlie had said the night before about coming into some money. Simon, suddenly realizing the enormity of what he had said, looked deeply mortified.

'How dare you!' exclaimed Charlie, his face a mask of fury. 'How dare you slander a respectable jeweller! What the hell do you know anyway? A merchant's boy from God knows where!'

'Now just a minute,' began Simon. He had still not regained his colour from before, but now he was looking very angry.

'What do you know about jewels anyway? And what are you insinuating? Are you suggesting that I . . .?' Yelden glared at them all, then turned on his heel. 'Devil take you all,' he shouted. 'I'm going out.'

'Charlie, when will you be back?' Dora asked in a puzzled tone.

'When I know I'm not going to be insulted in my own house,' he answered, his voice still raised. He went out, slamming the door behind him.

There was an embarrassed silence after he had gone, which was broken by Simon saying, 'I had better go too, my lady, leaving my apologies for distressing you.'

'Wait, Mr Grindle please,' said Dora, her voice not quite steady. 'Can you be certain . . . are you sure that those pearls are forgeries?'

He paused for a moment. 'It is as Lord Yelden says,' he said at last. 'I could be mistaken.' Again he paused, then took hold of Dora's hand. 'Believe me, my lady, I would do anything rather than distress you,' he said earnestly. For a moment, it seemed as though he might raise her hand to his lips, then he released it, bowed, said 'Good day to you,' and left.

As soon as the door had closed behind him, Dora started to sway as if she had been holding herself together until he had gone. Fenella hurried concernedly to her side and put her arm around her.

'Come, sit down here. I will send for some wine for you. Mama always recommends red wine if one feels faint.'

'Mama . . .' murmured Dora, then her face crumpled. 'Oh Nella, how I wish that Mama was here! How I wish we had never. . .'

'It was monstrous of him,' declared Fenella.

'Monstrous to subject you to such a scene!' They both knew that she was not referring to Simon Grindle.

A short time later, after Dora had calmed down and taken a few sips from the glass of rich red wine which Fenella had ordered, she said 'Nella, do *you* think that my pearls are forgeries?'

Fenella looked at her sister. Until they came to London, she had always seen it to be her task to protect her from any unpleasantness. As if Dora could read her mind, she went on, 'Don't hide anything from me, Nella. I need to know. How can I protect my baby's future if I don't understand the facts as they are?'

At this, Fenella said honestly, 'I don't know, Dora, but of this I am certain: Simon would never say such a thing unless he was sure of his opinions.'

At that moment, Dudley and Augusta arrived, and Fenella inwardly breathed a sigh of relief, thinking that their arrival would be a welcome diversion. Unfortunately, however, their appearance gave rise to an awkward moment which Fenella could not possibly have anticipated. They were talking idly about various acquaintances and their discussion had come round to Mr Grindle.

'He seems a very pleasant young man, although perhaps a little irresponsible,' said Dora, glancing at Fenella in a way that made her blush.

191

'He is very light-hearted, but I do not think that he is at all irresponsible with regard to important matters,' replied Dudley. 'I suppose he is enjoying the excitement of London society, of which he has had little experience, but he won't let it go to his head, I'm sure.'

'Is he intending to follow his father into his business?' Fenella asked.

'Yes, I believe so,' answered Dudley. 'In fact, he has already developed his own area of expertise and, in some matters, his father relies entirely upon his judgement.'

'And what area might that be?' Dora asked him.

'Well, his father deals with exports of luxury goods from the East, but Simon's particular interest is in gems and precious stones of all kinds.'

'The pearl ear-rings that I am wearing now, for instance,' said Augusta. 'Simon insisted on going with Dudley to buy them, so that he would not be cheated.'

'That was very kind of him,' said Dora in a colourless tone. There was an awkward silence and then Augusta began to speak about the ball that they were all to go to that evening. Soon afterwards, brother and sister left.

In an effort to divert Dora's attention, Fenella said, 'Why didn't you tell them about my engagement to Bev?'

'Because Mama and Papa do not know yet, of course,' she replied. 'Nella . . .' She paused for such a long time that Fenella wondered whether she was going to say anything more. Then at last she went on, 'Why do you think Charlie has . . . has sold my pearls?'

'It might not have been Charlie,' replied Fenella carefully. 'After all, Simon himself said that perhaps—'

'Oh Nella, don't be absurd,' said Dora sharply. 'What respectable jeweller would do such a thing? He would never be able to conduct any business in town again. And if you *dare* suggest that Papa would sink so low as to sell Grandmama's pearls, I shall scream.' She was silent for a long time, during which both of them contemplated the likelihood that Charlie was the one who had stooped low. Eventually, Dora said pitifully, 'Nella, why?'

Fenella thought hard. Now was not the moment to protect Dora from the truth. 'I believe that he may be gambling,' she said cautiously.

Dora sighed. 'I had half suspected it,' she said. 'All the evenings spent at his club, and the way that he always ends up in the card-room.' She sighed again. 'I do so wish we had never come to London. If only we could have stayed at Yelden Hall! But now it seems as though Charlie does not want us to go there at all.'

Although Dora had faced so bravely the possibility that Charlie might have sold her pearls, Fenella found it quite impossible even to suggest that Yelden Hall itself might be in danger. 'He did say that he would take you to the seaside,' she reminded Dora. 'That was kind of him.'

Dora nodded. 'The sea air will do us both good,' she replied, patting her stomach.

'Of course it will.' Fenella put her arm around her sister. 'Charlie loves you very much and he always will. I'm sure of it,' she said. 'As far as the pearls are concerned, maybe there is a perfectly simple explanation. Just one dishonest shop-assistant or something.'

Dora nodded; neither of them believed what she had said.

CHAPTER FIFTEEN

Charlie came back later in the day, for when Fenella went to her sister's room to make sure that she was all right, she heard voices inside. Thinking that Dora might just be talking to her abigail, she pushed the door open in time to hear Charlie say, 'Dora my dear, you know I would never do anything to hurt you . . .'

Fenella just caught her sister saying, 'Then why did you . . .' before she softly closed the door. She would make a very bad third in that scene and she had a horror of eavesdropping. She could only hope that her sister and her husband would be able to resolve their differences.

Certainly when Fenella met them downstairs later, peace seemed to have been restored. Charlie looked very much the proud father-to-be, and Dora, if not looking as happy as Fenella had ever seen her, at least appeared to be at ease.

'Are you sure that you are well enough to o out, Dora?' Fenella asked her sister concernedly.

'Of course I am,' Dora answered brightly.

'But this ball must be your last,' insisted Charlie. 'You must not risk any harm to the baby—or to yourself, of course. I insist upon it.'

This harmony between husband and wife seemed to get the evening off to a propitious start, despite the fact that the air felt heavy and oppressive.

'I should not be surprised if we had a storm,' Charlie remarked, as they left the house.

'Well if there is going to be one, I hope it comes quickly,' replied Dora. 'I find this heavy atmosphere very enervating.'

'Then why not stay at home?' suggested Charlie. 'I will escort Fenella and then you may be easy.'

Dora hesitated, her foot on the step of the carriage, then she said determinedly, 'No, Charlie, my mind is made up. I shall go, but this will be the very last ball I attend until after baby is born.'

'As you wish, my love,' answered Charlie.

Fenella wondered what explanation he had given Dora and whether his wife's presence meant that he would keep away from the card-room. If that were so, then he was clearly facing the prospect with equanimity.

The ball was at the home of Sir Wilfred and Lady Brewster, which was situated in Hanover Square, quite close to the Yeldens' house. As they travelled, Dora and Charlie made desultory conversation, and Fenella thought about the vexed question of her engagement. Of one thing she could be thankful: only a handful of people knew about it, so it would not be a topic of conversation at the ball that evening. She really did not want to talk about the matter when she had not yet decided what to do about it.

She wondered how Bev had got on with Mama and Papa. It would not be the first time that they had met him of course, for he had been at Dora's wedding. There was a faint possibility that he might come to the Brewsters' that evening, although Fenella thought it more likely that he would dine at Brightstones and ride back much later. On the other hand, he might fail to appear that evening, not because he had been delayed, but because he did not want to see her. After all, he had offered for her hand out of chivalry, and not because he actually wanted to marry her. Furthermore, she could not forget that he had gambled with Charlie. Perhaps he had even won from the earl some of the proceeds of Dora's necklace? Somehow, that made the whole matter seem much more serious.

These latter thoughts were so depressing that she was very glad when Dora called her attention to the fact that they had arrived at the Brewsters' and it was time to alight. They were among the last arrivals and Sir Wilfred and his lady were on the point of leaving their post at the head of the stairs.

'My dear Lady Yelden,' purred Lady Brewster. 'I am delighted that you felt able to come. I am told that this is to be your last engagement.'

'I fear so,' replied Dora.

'And are you to retire to the country?' Lady Brewster went on. 'Yelden Hall is very beautiful, I believe.'

'Charlie is to take me to the sea,' said Dora. 'We'll go on to Yelden Hall later, I expect.' Fenella was too busy responding to Sir Wilfred's greeting to be able to see how Charlie had reacted to those words, or to take in Dora's expression whilst she was speaking.

The rooms were already full and the little party from Curzon Street soon split up, each one claimed by different acquaintances. Fenella had barely entered the room when Simon Grindle approached her.

'I say, I'm very sorry if I put you in an awkward situation earlier on,' he said. 'But I . . . that is to say . . .' He stopped awkwardly, realizing that his explanations were not getting him anywhere.

'It's all right,' said Fenella. 'You can tell me the truth.' She dropped her voice. 'Are you sure that those pearls are forgeries?'

'As sure as I can be,' he answered in a similarly low tone. 'I may be just a merchant's boy, but I do know something about the subject.' The lines about his mouth hardened and Fenella remembered how Dudley had told her that Simon had been bullied at school because of his background.

'It's all right,' she said again, in soothing tones. 'I think that perhaps you frightened Charlie, or he would never have spoken to you in such a way.' She halted, suddenly aware of what she had betrayed.

This time, it was Simon's turn to reassure her. 'As soon as I saw them in the box, I guessed what had happened,' he told her. 'He won't have been the first nobleman to have sold his wife's jewellery without her knowledge.' He paused briefly. 'Perhaps I shouldn't say this, but is it, as I suspect, that he is gambling to excess?'

Fenella nodded, relieved. 'That was why I wanted to go to Ranelagh—to confirm my suspicions that that was what he was doing.' It was her turn to pause. 'I suppose that the Hall is sold by now?'

Simon inclined his head. 'Charlie was very pressing, and my father was eager to buy. I

198

delayed the business for as long as I could.' They were silent for a few moments, then Simon said intensely, 'How can she bear it?'

Fenella did not need to ask of whom he was speaking. 'She loves him,' she replied simply. She looked up into his face, and saw on it for a few seconds an expression of such distress that she was forced to wonder whether he had fallen in love with Dora himself. If he had, then he was doomed to disappointment. Dora would never indulge in any kind of illicit liaison, even if she ceased to love Charlie. Her principles were far too high for that. But Fenella could not help wondering for how long Dora's love for Charlie would survive if he failed to mend his ways. Those very principles of hers would be deeply injured by the knowledge that Charlie had behaved towards her in such an underhand manner.

As the evening went on and Bev did not appear, Fenella was forced to conclude that either he was staying with her parents or he was deliberately avoiding her. She tried hard not to speculate about which might be the more likely.

At around eleven, Fenella encountered her sister and thought that she was looking as if she was flagging a little.

'Would you like to go home?' she asked her. 'Shall I go and find Charlie for you?'

'By no means,' declared Dora. 'I shall feel better directly. But I must say, I would not mind a little more to eat. Mrs Yarmouth was demanding so much of my attention at supper that I found it difficult to consume anything.'

'Why not go back to the supper-room, then?' suggested Fenella. 'I'll go with you.'

They went together and found that the supper-room was now very quiet compared to the hubbub that had reigned earlier. A few people were scattered here and there. In a corner seated close together at one of the tables were Charlie and Mrs Maxfield. They were quite alone. Dora paused in the doorway, a frozen expression on her face.

It was left to Fenella to call out in a way which her mother would instantly have condemned as juvenile and gauche, 'Charlie! Mrs Maxfield! You too have felt hungry again, I see.'

If Mrs Maxfield felt any guilt about being discovered alone with her friend's husband, she did not betray it, but merely said in her usual vivacious manner, 'Lady Yelden! Miss Parrish! Yes, I have danced so much that I have worked up a second appetite, and Charlie has been doing much the same thing by gambling in the card-room. Stephen would not come, so Charlie has taken pity on me. Is it not good-natured of him?'

Dora did not say anything, but smiled and walked forward. Fenella, walking beside her, discovered that she could only recall seeing Mrs Maxfield dancing on one occasion, and that had been with Charlie.

'Charlie has just been telling me that you are to go to the seaside when your baby is born,' Mrs Maxfield went on brightly, when they were all sitting down. 'How delightful that will be!'

'Yes, I am looking forward to it very much,' said Dora calmly. 'Charlie says that we are to go to Lyme Regis.'

'Lyme is very healthy, I believe,' remarked Mrs Maxfield. 'Who knows, perhaps you will decide to buy property there?'

'I hardly think so,' said Charlie repressively.

'But with Yelden Hall sold—'

'You are mistaken,' interrupted Dora. 'There is no question of selling Yelden Hall, is there, Charlie?' She looked at her husband's face and at once saw the truth written there. 'Charlie?' she repeated, in a bewildered tone.

'Oh for God's sake, it's only bricks and mortar,' he declared angrily, getting to his feet. Fenella noticed that he avoided his wife's eyes.

'How could you make such a decision without telling me?' exclaimed Dora, also rising.

'There's no reason why I should,' stormed Charlie. 'It is mine to dispose of and I do not need to refer to you.'

Dora took a deep breath. 'It is *not* just yours, Charlie,' she declared, her voice shaking with emotion. 'It belonged to your father, and should belong to your sons and grandsons as

201

much as it belongs to you.'

He whitened. 'How dare you lecture me?' he demanded.

'I dare because I am your wife and I am carrying your child,' she retorted. 'For what do you need the money, Charlie? So that you can throw good after bad across the gaming-tables, just as you did with the money from my pearls?'

He raised his hand, and for one dreadful moment it seemed as if he might strike her. His hand dropped to his side; they stared at one another for a long moment, both looking equally horrified; then he threw his chair to one side, overturning it, and stalked from the room.

Dora stood completely still, then began to sway, and both Fenella and Mrs Maxfield sprang forward to help her back into her chair.

Fenella glared at the other woman, who said at once, 'I had no idea that she did not know. Please believe me, Miss Parrish.'

Fenella sighed. 'It makes no difference now, does it? Help me to make my sister comfortable, then would you have the goodness to ask our carriage to be sent for? I must take her home at once.'

'And Charlie?' murmured Mrs Maxfield.

'Charlie has done enough damage for one evening,' retorted Fenella sharply. 'He can perfectly well look after himself.'

Dora said nothing either before the carriage

was brought, or whilst they were travelling back. Once they were in the hall of the house in Curzon Street, however, she turned to her sister and said 'Get my maid to put some of my things together and the things for the baby. I'm going home.'

'Home?' ventured Fenella.

'To Mama, of course,' answered Dora sharply. 'What other home do I have? This is not ours, and neither is Yelden Hall, it seems.'

'But Dora, to travel in your condition . . .'

'Nella, I *will* go,' insisted her sister, her voice rising on a note of hysteria. 'Will you make arrangements for me, or must I do so for myself?'

Perceiving that the first necessity was to keep her sister calm, Fenella said, 'Of course I will help you. Come and sit down while I get things organized.' She ran upstairs and rang for Dora's maid and gave her her instructions.

The maid was strangely unsurprised by the nature of the order, although she did find the timing of it a little odd. 'Plenty of women want to be with their mothers at such times,' she said. 'Reckon her ladyship's no different. But wouldn't it be better to wait till the morning, miss?'

'Yes, it would,' agreed Fenella frankly. 'But she won't wait. Ladies in my sister's condition get strange fancies, don't they?'

That done, Fenella was obliged to make shift for herself with her packing, for Millie

203

was laid up with a very heavy cold. She was not sorry to be without her. Millie's previous performance as a conspirator did not encourage her to hope for great things, and after all, what she did not know, she could not reveal.

When they got into the carriage the storm had not yet broken and the air was more heavy and oppressive than ever. As Dora climbed in, her maid whispered to Fenella, 'Do you think my lady's baby will be born on the journey, miss?'

'I hope not,' replied Fenella fervently in the same whispered tone.

The journey through the darkened streets and then on into the countryside seemed interminable. Dora sat with her eyes shut whilst Jane watched her anxiously, and Fenella wondered when the storm would break and give them some relief.

They were still a short distance from Hounslow when they heard a shout, and their carriage came to a halt.

'Highwaymen!' breathed Dora in horrified tones, then she gave a little gasp and gripped her stomach.

'Oh, my Lord!' wailed Jane.

'Highwaymen!' exclaimed Fenella indignantly. 'That's all we need!' She drew down the window. The wind had started to get up and a few drops of rain were falling. A shadowed figure walked over to the door. He had no chance to speak before Fenella declared, 'For goodness' sake go away, you stupid man! We have no money to give you and my sister needs to get home without loss of time in order to have her baby in safety.'

'Then you were ill-advised to set out tonight,' was the reply. As he came into the light cast by the lantern, she saw that it was Bev.

'Oh Bev, thank goodness,' exclaimed Fenella, forgetting the embarrassment of being confronted with the man to whom she had just become engaged in the relief of having someone to help her shoulder the burden. 'It was not our choice,' she went on.

'Then whose?' he asked challengingly.

Ignoring his words, Fenella said, 'We must be on our way.' Before she could say any more, however, she was interrupted by a cry from Dora. Instantly she caught hold of Dora's hand and found her grip returned convulsively.

'Nella,' panted Dora, as soon as she was able. 'I . . . I don't think that . . . that we will get to . . . to Mama.'

Fenella turned to look at Bev. 'What can we do?' she said.

'I passed a farmhouse only a few hundred yards back,' he replied. 'I think that we had better go there. I'll ride ahead and rouse them and I'll tell your carriage to follow on. And for goodness' sake, stop that woman from having hysterics if you can.'

Jane was indeed sobbing in rather an alarming manner.

'Be quiet at once,' Fenella said sharply, 'or I shall make you ride on the box. I do not care how hard it rains, you shall *not* distress her ladyship.' At this, Jane's sobbing subsided to a general sniffing sound and Fenella could only hope that the maid would be able to make herself useful in ways which did not have anything to do with childbirth.

It was with great relief that Fenella felt the carriage draw to a halt in front of the isolated farmhouse. Dora had cried out several more times and on each occasion she had needed to grip her sister's hands. These occasions had become more and more frequent and Fenella had begun to think that her sister might give birth in the carriage itself. At least, she decided, now that they had arrived at the house there would be someone there who would be used to the birth of young creatures, even if they were only calves, foals or lambs!

As she helped her sister down from the carriage, Bev hurried from the shelter of the lighted doorway carrying a cloak in his hands, and he held it over them as they walked to the house, for it was now raining hard.

'Thank God,' declared Fenella fervently. 'Where is the farmer's wife? She must conduct my sister to a bed-chamber at once.'

Dora was crying out again now, bending over and gripping her sister's hand.

'There is no farmer's wife,' said Bev, quietly.

'Well sister, then, it doesn't matter who,' replied Fenella, giving him only half her attention.

'You don't understand,' answered Bev. 'There is no one here. The house is deserted.'

CHAPTER SIXTEEN

At last, now, Fenella gave Bev her full attention. 'Then we must go elsewhere,' she said anxiously.

'There is nowhere else to go,' he answered. 'That is, nowhere that's near enough. Your sister is far too near her time for her to be moved, or so it seems to me. And look at the weather! The storm has only just begun and may well get far worse before it is over. If you travel on now, you might easily have her giving birth in the carriage. At least this house is clean and dry and it appears to be fully furnished.' He turned to Jane. 'Come with me, wench. You can help prepare a room for her ladyship.'

Once Jane had been given a task to do, she became much more efficient and when Fenella had succeeded in helping her sister upstairs, she found that Jane had made the bed.

'The sheets are aired, my lady,' said the girl, 'so you can get in immediately.'

The coachman carried Dora's box upstairs and Jane helped her ladyship out of her things. For a brief moment, Fenella watched Jane unfastening Dora's ball gown, and recalled how just a short time ago they had got ready to go to the Brewsters'. Then, pulling herself together, she searched in the box and found a night-gown for Dora. That done, she hurried downstairs and saw that Bev's groom was lighting the fire whilst Bev looked for provisions.

'Where is the coachman?' she asked.

'He and your groom are stabling the horses,' answered Bev. 'There doesn't seem to be a great deal of food here.'

He sounded surprisingly optimistic, and Fenella could not help answering rather sharply, 'You don't need to sound so pleased.'

He turned from his task and looked straight at her. 'A well-equipped, deserted house full of provisions and not far from Hounslow Heath would give me grave cause for concern,' he replied.

She looked at him and shivered. 'You think that this may be a highwayman's house?' she asked him anxiously.

He shook his head. 'As I said, too little food about—no bread, for example. I think someone left this house, certainly very recently—perhaps for personal reasons. But just in case, Rusty can keep guard at the front, and—'

At that point, a great cry was heard from upstairs.

'Your sister,' said Bev.

'I know,' replied Fenella.

'You should go to her,' he reminded her.

'I know,' she said again, but still she hesitated. 'Bev, who is going to deliver this baby?'

He took hold of her hand. 'You'll have to do it,' he told her. 'There is no one else.' She stared at him aghast, but in all truth, he was not telling her anything that she did not already know. He sighed. 'Come on, someone's got to help her and that maidservant of hers is worse than useless.'

He had only just finished speaking when the coachman and groom came in, brushing down their coats and stamping their feet.

'You two, get warm and dry, but make sure the back door and the windows are secured,' said Bev.

They went upstairs to find Dora lying in bed, clutching at the bedclothes, her face and hair bathed with perspiration. Jane was standing as far away as possible, wringing her hands.

'You, go and find the baby's clothes together with towels and blankets,' Bev said to her. 'Then you might see what you can do about procuring drinks for everyone.'

Glad to be given a task which did not involve her staying while the baby was born,

Jane disappeared with alacrity.

Bev grinned ruefully. 'You mustn't blame her: she hasn't been trained for this kind of activity.'

'Neither have I,' Fenella reminded him.

'No, but you are ten times the woman that she is. In any case, you are Lady Yelden's sister. You cannot desert her now.'

'You are right, I cannot, and I don't intend to.' Later, she would remember the compliment that he had paid her, but for now there was no time. She went over to sit on the bed close to her sister. 'Are the pains very frequent now, Dora?' she asked.

Dora nodded. 'It seems . . . as if . . . there is barely any gap . . .' she panted; then the next one was upon her.

'Lady Yelden,' Bev said, as soon as she was able to listen again, 'I fear that I must give your sister assistance. I have no wish to embarrass you, but there is no one else.'

'I don't care, I don't care,' answered Dora passionately. 'I just want it to be born.'

Dora's baby was born half an hour later, a fine healthy boy who cried as soon as he emerged. In the end, it was Fenella who helped her nephew into the world, whilst Bev sat at Dora's head giving her encouragement. It was he who cut the cord, and then summoned Jane to bring water and a towel to wash the baby; and clean linen to wrap him in.

As Dora received her baby, she looked tired

but happy and as beautiful as a woman could look under such adverse circumstances.

Now that the baby had been born and all was clean and tidy once more, Jane came into her own. 'Why don't you both go and have something to eat and drink downstairs?' she suggested. 'My lady and I will manage very well now.'

'Nella,' came Dora's voice from the bed. Fenella walked over to her sister's side, and bent so that Dora could kiss her. 'Thank you. And you too, sir.'

Bev bowed with something approaching his usual grace. 'To say that it was a pleasure would perhaps be overstating the case,' he admitted. 'But it was certainly a privilege.'

They left the room, but as soon as Bev had closed the door behind them, the enormity of what had taken place struck Fenella and she began to shake. 'Bev,' she whispered. 'Bev, we *did* it.'

He laughed and gathered her into his arms, and it seemed like the most natural thing in the world. 'We certainly did,' he said eventually. 'I am engaged to a remarkable woman.' They drew apart, then he bent his head and kissed her on the mouth, lingeringly and with tenderness.

The sound of voices below broke into their private world.

'We must tell everyone else that all is well,' Bev said. 'One of the men must go with a message for Lord Yelden. Then we certainly ought to get some sleep.'

'Sleep?' queried Fenella. 'What time is it, then?'

'About six o'clock in the morning,' said Bev with a grin. 'An eventful night, wasn't it?'

*   *   *

Even though it was after six o'clock when Fenella finally got to bed, she found it impossible to sleep later than ten o'clock. She got out of bed and stood for a few moments in indecision, very much wanting to get some water for washing, but not sure where to go. She put her head around the door, and by great good fortune, Jane happened to be passing at that point so she was able to make her needs known.

Jane hurried away and by the time she came back, Fenella had found clean clothes and put them out on the bed. The maid picked up the things that she had used the previous day. 'I'll wash these along with my lady's things,' she said. 'The storm's passed, and it's a lovely day.'

Fenella looked out of the window. The sun was shining brightly, making the puddles sparkle. She realized that the threatened storm had broken in the night and blown itself out, but with all that had happened she had not been aware of it at all, apart from the first few minutes when they had hurried inside from the carriage.

As soon as she was dressed, she went to see her sister. The scene that met her eyes was very different from that in which she had played her part the night before. Dora was sitting up in bed dressed in a clean night-gown, and she looked absolutely radiant. Standing beside the bed was Bev, also in clean linen, and he was holding the baby in his arms, and looking down at him with an expression that was a mixture of awe and tenderness. This was how things should be, Fenella told herself, but it ought to be Charlie standing there looking like a proud father, and not Bev. For a brief moment, Fenella felt that she was witnessing an everyday domestic scene in which she could play no part, and as she looked at the little group she was conscious of a stab of envy.

Then Dora turned towards her and said 'Oh Nella, come and see. He's absolutely beautiful,' and the strange feeling was gone as Fenella hurried forward to look at her new nephew.

'Take him,' Bev said, and passed the baby to her. Fenella stood looking down at him in wonderment. The tiny baby was fast asleep, quite unaware of all the upheaval for which he had been responsible.

'He's perfect,' she breathed.

'I'll leave you together and go down for my breakfast,' Bev said, leaving the room and closing the door softly behind him.

'Isn't he beautiful?' Dora said again, after Bev had gone.

'Yes, he is,' agreed Fenella. 'Have you decided what to call him?'

'He must be called Charles, of course, after his father. But do you think that I might call him after Mr Beville too? After all,' she went on with a blush, 'he did help to . . . to deliver him, in a way.'

'Charles Giles,' said Fenella thoughtfully; then she said it again to be sure that she knew how it would sound. 'Two names ending in 's' sounds rather strange, really. How about putting *Humphrey* in the middle—for Papa?'

'He doesn't *look* like a Humphrey,' Dora said critically. They both looked at the baby and giggled.

'What about Charles Beville?' suggested Fenella eventually. 'After all, no one calls him Giles; he's always known as Bev.'

'Charles Beville,' said the new mother thoughtfully. 'Yes, that sounds well, doesn't it?'

A short time later, Fenella came downstairs to the agreeable smell of bacon cooking. Bev's groom had been to Hounslow to collect supplies and, as she took in the pleasing savoury aroma, she remembered that she had not eaten since supper-time and her mouth began to water.

Bev was in the kitchen, and as she looked at him she suddenly recalled how they had kissed earlier that morning, and she felt absurdly shy.

He greeted her very naturally, however, and invited her to be seated. 'You and I were very busy last night and we deserve a good breakfast,' he said.

She looked around more carefully and noticed that it was Bev's groom who was cooking the bacon. Bev followed the direction of her gaze and said, 'I first met Rusty in the army when he was my batman. I do believe there's no end to the things he can turn his hand to.'

'Not true,' commented Rusty, as he deftly served the bacon on to two plates. 'Delivering that there baby would've been quite beyond me.' He put one plate in front of Fenella. 'Now get round the outside of that, miss, and you'll be a new man—if you'll pardon the expression.'

'Thank you,' said Fenella laughing.

She watched Bev as he tucked into his breakfast with whole-hearted enjoyment. It occurred to her that part of his attraction lay in the fact that he seemed to be at home in so many different situations. Her own father was most comfortable in the role of country squire, but he often seemed ill-at-ease at social gatherings, and his way of dealing with domestic crises was to ride to the other end of his estate as quickly as possible.

By way of contrast, however, the night before, Bev had been first the man of action, and then the resourceful person upon whom everyone had depended. This morning, he had held a newly born baby like an expert, and now he seemed utterly relaxed at the kitchen table in his shirt sleeves, his dark hair caught back with a ribbon. His appearance could not have been in greater contrast to that first night when he had appeared at the ball in Cookham in his paint and powder, silks and satins, and yet he had the ability to be equally at home in either setting.

At once she realized that she had been staring at him like a yokel, her knife and fork in her hands whilst for his part, he was regarding her with quizzical amusement. Blushing, she looked down at her plate and turned her attention to her breakfast.

After they had eaten, Bev invited her to go outside for some fresh air. It was not until they were outside that she realized that this was the first time that she had stepped out of the house since their arrival the previous night. The house appeared to have very little garden apart from an orchard with plentiful fruit trees. They looked well cared for and it seemed to Fenella, eyeing them critically as the countrywoman that she was, that there would be a good crop.

'Rusty made enquiries in the town,' Bev told her, as they strolled around the orchard and then out of the side entrance to the front of the house. 'Apparently, this place has been occupied by a very respectable couple, who would be horrified at the very idea of having anything to do with highwaymen. The wife's mother became ill only a few days ago, and they have gone to care for her. The general opinion locally seems to be that they will be quite satisfied if we leave the place in good order, replace what we have used and put a sum of money at their disposal. But I'll also leave one of my cards so that they can refer to me if necessary.'

They strolled in silence for a little while. 'How soon do you think Charlie will be here?' Fenella said eventually.

Bev shook his head. 'I cannot say,' he replied. 'I could only send the coachman to look for him, starting first, of course, in Curzon Street. I wish with all my heart that I could have written him a note explaining the situation, but there appear to be no writing materials in the house. I hope the coachman will be able to give a message which will tell Charlie what he needs to know without alarming him.' He paused for a moment then went on, 'Why did you leave London at that hour and in such weather? It was sheer madness to set out in such a way with your sister in her condition.'

'I'm afraid that Dora found out about Charlie's selling the Hall,' said Fenella. 'It was such a shock to her that she insisted upon setting off to be with Mama. There was nothing I could do to prevent her, so I did the one thing that I could do, which was to insist that I accompany her. Did I do wrong?'

He shook his head. 'You did all that you could do,' he said. 'Is it definite that he is to sell the Hall, then? I remember your letting slip the fact that it was mortgaged.'

'I fear it is sold already,' she replied, her head high. 'But you of all people must know why.'

He wrinkled his brow. 'I don't know why you should say so,' he said.

'You gamble with him,' Fenella pointed out.

'Not really,' he answered her.

'Bev, I *saw* you,' she protested. 'You were gambling with him at Ranelagh. There was money at your elbow—money won from him, no doubt.'

He had been leaning negligently against a gate post. Now he stood up straight. 'And what is that supposed to mean?' he asked her, drawing his brows together. 'It almost sounds as if you blame me for his weakness.'

'I don't blame you for it, but I do think that you took advantage of it to win money from him hand over fist,' she said assertively.

'You really think me capable of that?' he asked her. They stared at one another in silence. Before either of them could break it, either for good or ill, there was a sound of hoofbeats, and Charlie came into view, followed by the groom. As soon as he reached them, he leaped down from the saddle, and thrust his horse's reins into the hands of his groom.

He strode towards Bev ignoring Fenella completely, his chin thrust forward, and began to speak without any preamble whatsoever. 'What the devil do you mean by it?' he demanded aggressively. 'Why the hell have you dragged my wife out here to have my child in this benighted spot?'

If Charlie had forgotten the courtesies, then Bev certainly had not. He bowed politely, and said, 'Give you good day, Yelden. I can assure you that to bring your wife here was not my idea.'

'Then whose idea was it?' demanded Charlie. 'Let me tell you that I hold you entirely to blame for this sorry affair. If she has come to harm through this adventure, then there will be a reckoning between us.' He waved his crop threateningly at Bev.

Fenella decided that it was time for her to intervene. 'Dora has not come to any harm at all,' she said soothingly. 'And your son is the most beautiful baby that anyone ever saw. Why don't you come and see them now?'

Charlie glared at Bev, then allowed her to lead him into the house. Bev stayed outside, taking the sunshine. When Fenella emerged some time later, he was waiting for her, but this time, his groom was standing holding their horses ready a short distance away.

'I think everything will be all right now,' she

said. 'Dora had the sense not to tell Charlie that you were actually there when the baby was born, and none of the servants know for sure. But Bev—'

'Don't tell me,' he interrupted. 'You think that the most tactful thing that I could do would be to depart and, as you can see, I have already anticipated you.'

'Do you mind?' Fenella said diffidently. 'I really think it would be better for Charlie and Dora.'

'And for you?' he put in. She recalled the accusations that she had made, and blushed, but she returned his gaze squarely. 'Perhaps I do owe you an explanation of some kind,' he said. 'I *have* gambled with Charlie on the odd occasion, but strangely enough, winning money "hand over fist", as you put it, from men considerably younger and less experienced than myself, has never appealed to me. Incidentally, my favourite game is piquet, as anyone who knows me well will tell you, and I don't think that it's a game that Charlie plays.'

She was silent. Eventually he said, 'Nothing to say? Don't you even want to accuse me of raising the money for your engagement ring from my winnings?' She looked into his face, and saw that he looked angry and bitterly hurt. Before she could say anything that might put things right, however, he said, 'Perhaps it would be as well for there to be a little distance between us, at least for a time, so that neither of us is tempted to say anything that might be beyond forgiveness.' In marked contrast to his words, he drew closer to her, and took her hand. 'By the way, you did very well; very well indeed.'

'No,' she murmured. 'No, I didn't.'

'Not a debutante in a thousand could have done what you did,' he said. He took her hand and looked down at it. 'You're a remarkable young woman, but you must learn to trust me.' Then he raised her hand to his lips, kissed it briefly, and mounted his horse, which Rusty had been holding for him.

'Until our next meeting,' he said, and rode away.

After he had gone, she raised her hand to her cheek. She could not decide what to think about him. The hurt that he had shown at her accusations had undoubtedly been real. She had seen him gambling and carousing and meeting actresses, but she had also seen that he could be resourceful, gentle and compassionate. Which was the real Bev?

CHAPTER SEVENTEEN

Fenella never found out exactly what had passed between Dora and Charlie, but when she next saw him, he was every inch the proud father, very ready to hold his newborn son with his wife's help. She did notice, however, that he did not seem nearly as adept as Bev, who had appeared to know almost by instinct how to hold a baby safely.

'I have decided what to name him,' Dora said to her husband in her sister's presence. 'He is to be called Charles Beville.'

Charlie frowned a little. 'I don't see why he should be named after that fellow,' he grumbled.

'But Charlie, Mr Beville is your friend,' Dora replied reasonably. 'After all, it was he who came to our rescue last night and found us this lodging; and remember, he is also to be your brother-in-law.'

'I suppose so,' Charlie answered grudgingly. 'If it had been a girl, we could have called it after Fenella,' he went on, brightening. 'After all, she did deliver the baby.'

'Yes she did, and all by herself, too,' agreed Dora. 'We both owe her a debt of gratitude.' Fenella did not need the warning glance that Dora threw in her direction. She had never thought that it would be politic to reveal Bev's intimate involvement in the delivery of the baby.

Doctor Driver arrived during the afternoon, having made a special journey to visit his patient. He congratulated the new parents on their fine son, and also had some generous words of praise for Fenella.

'Such a pity that the career of physician is not a profession open to a lady,' he said. 'I could make excellent use of you, Miss Parrish.'

After a careful examination, the doctor pronounced that although under normal circumstances, it would be desirable for her ladyship to remain in bed for a week, since they were away from home she might be transported back to the Curzon Street house with care.

'But can we not go and see Mama and Papa since we are already part way there?' pleaded Dora.

'Your father is still not yet completely recovered,' Charlie pointed out. 'And besides, the journey is twice as far. I am sure that Dr Driver would not advise it.'

Taking his cue from his noble client, the doctor nodded in agreement. 'There will be plenty of time for paying family visits later,' he said. 'Why not suggest that Sir Humphrey and Lady Parrish come to town to see their new grandson?'

'We shall be removing to Lyme Regis quite soon,' said Charlie quickly. 'There will probably not be enough time.'

'Ah, sea air! Just the thing,' declared the doctor. 'That will soon put the roses back in your cheeks, Lady Yelden.'

Dora agreed rather forlornly. Whilst Charlie was taking the doctor to his gig, Fenella said to her sister, 'Do you want to see

223

Mama and Papa?'

Dora nodded. 'More than anything, but Charlie obviously doesn't want them to come. I expect he's afraid that they will learn about his sale of Yelden Hall and challenge him about it, but they are bound to hear about it some time. He can't hide it for ever.'

'Perhaps he wants to wait until it is a *fait accompli*,' answered Fenella. 'Was there no alternative to selling the Hall, then?'

Dora shook her head. 'Charlie says that the estate was already encumbered when he came into possession of it. His gambling has been to try and recoup some of the losses incurred by his father, but his efforts have been unsuccessful, I'm afraid.' She sighed. 'If only I had known from the very beginning what the situation was, then I could have told him that we would all stay in the country and make savings in that way. But Charlie says that he wanted me to enjoy London life.'

'Do you mind very much; about the Hall, I mean?' Fenella asked her cautiously.

'It's never been my home,' replied Dora. 'I mind for baby Charles because it should have been his birthright. More than that, I mind that Charlie did not tell me. But the main thing is that he should be sorry for what he has done, and that he should cease from gambling, and this he has promised to do.'

Fenella smiled and said nothing. She wanted to be pleased for her sister, but she could not shake off a feeling of grave disquiet. Going by what she had seen over the past weeks, it seemed to her to be far more likely that Charlie himself had wanted to be in London, than that he had wanted to take his wife there. And Dora's assertion that Charlie had renounced his gambling habits did not convince her. A man who was capable of selling his wife's pearls and his own home in order to finance his gambling had a very serious problem, which one little promise was not going to solve.

As soon as the doctor had gone, Charlie set about making arrangements to have Dora taken back to London in all comfort. Since this could not be arranged satisfactorily until the next day, they were obliged to stay in the farmhouse for one more night. Charlie occupied the room that Bev had had, and proved himself to be very attentive to his wife and child.

Whilst pleased at this situation, Fenella found herself feeling rather low and dispirited. At first she put it down to tiredness, but eventually, she was forced to admit that she was missing Bev. What was more, with everything that had happened, she had had no real chance to speak to him about their engagement, or to ask him how things had gone with her mother and father.

She was glad to be able to distract herself by travelling into Hounslow with Bridge,

Charlie's groom, and buying sufficient provisions to last them until the next day. Once in Hounslow, they hired a gig, in order to bring back the things that they had bought. She remembered that it had been Bev's groom who had cooked breakfast for them and asked Bridge if he could cook.

'Not at all, miss,' he replied, grinning. 'Leastways, not unless you want to be poisoned.'

That discovery made, Fenella had the great forethought to order some cooked food to be delivered to the farmhouse that evening. 'We can always warm it up when it arrives, if we have a good fire going,' she told Bridge.

Thanks to Fenella's enterprise, therefore, they all succeeded in eating reasonably well until their return to London.

Once back there, Dora made a rapid recovery. Baby Charles was very much admired and Charlie was very willing to boast about him to all his acquaintances, but after the novelty of fatherhood had worn off, he did not appear to stay at home any more than before. Dora did not comment upon this, but Fenella noted the return of the look of anxiety which crossed her brow all too frequently.

Among the first callers was Mrs Maxfield, accompanied by Bev. Mrs Maxfield was strangely diffident about holding the baby but Bev, perhaps rendered confident by his previous success, took the young lord capably in his arms and walked about the room with him. Watching his eyes meet those of Dora above the baby's head, Fenella remembered seeing him hold the baby at the inn and she was once more conscious of a pang of jealousy. After all, she told herself, Dora had always been beautiful, and motherhood seemed to have given her an added glow. It would not be at all surprising if Bev found himself attracted to her.

'What a very romantic story it was,' Mrs Maxfield declared, breaking into Fenella's thoughts. 'You running off in the middle of the night and meeting Bev, who rescued you! What on earth made you set off so suddenly?'

'A woman cannot help but long for her mother at such a time,' Dora replied calmly, but Fenella, sensing a slight tension in her bearing, remembered how it had been Mrs Maxfield's indiscretion with regard to the sale of Yelden Hall that had made Dora take flight from London in the first place.

'And so you are to come and join us at our country residence in Devon,' Mrs Maxfield went on. 'How very agreeable that will be. I quite long to get to know little Charles better.'

Dora wrinkled her brow in response to her visitor's words. 'I think not,' she replied. 'Charlie is arranging to take me and baby to Lyme Regis to enjoy the sea air.'

'Oh no, that plan is quite changed,' declared Mrs Maxfield confidently. 'You are all going to join us at Cliff House. You can very well visit the sea from there, you know, and we will be such a merry party. Charlie was enraptured with the idea.'

'You are letting your enthusiasm run away with you, my dear cousin,' said Bev, handing the baby back to Dora. 'You must not speak of it as a fixed thing. Charlie will certainly not want to make such an arrangement without consulting his wife.'

Mrs Maxfield flushed a little, but merely said, 'As to that, a man may arrange a delightful surprise for his wife, surely.' But after this, she left the subject, and talked of other matters until the end of the visit.

'Nella, do you think that Charlie has really arranged for us to go to Cliff House without asking me?' Dora asked her sister, almost before the door had closed properly behind the visitors.

Privately, Fenella thought that a man who had sold his house from over his wife's head was probably capable of anything, but she merely said, 'You have seen how Mrs Maxfield's tongue runs on; I expect she does not always hear properly what is being said, owing to the sound of her own voice.'

Dora smiled, but said, 'Well, I shall ask him about it later.'

That evening, Dora tackled Charlie about what Mrs Maxfield had said. He had come to see her in her room before going out. Looking at him, Dora thought how he had changed over the past two years. Along with any hint of country simplicity, he had lost his healthy complexion, and now looked rather pale; and there were lines developing at the corners of his eyes and round his mouth. He had also put on weight.

'Oh yes,' he agreed airily. 'I thought how much more agreeable it would be for you to be there with friends. The Lyme Regis scheme was never a fixed thing, you know! Not fixed at all! And besides, I should not have been able to stay with you for the whole visit at Lyme, whereas at Cliff House, we shall be together all the time.'

Dora looked disappointed. 'But I had quite thought that it would be a lovely, peaceful summer, just the two of us and the baby.'

'Well yes, but you could hardly expect . . .' he began, then halted, running his finger inside his collar as if it were a little tight. 'Believe me, you will be much happier with the Maxfields.'

'I do not know whether I shall,' replied Dora colouring, her chin high. 'I'm afraid that I do not really care for Mrs Maxfield very much.'

'Oh for heaven's sake,' Charlie interrupted, reddening. 'A delightful woman like Connie does you a kindness and all you can do is carp and criticize. I declare, you would be very well served if I just packed you off back to Cookham to your mother!'

'I wish you would,' flashed Dora. 'I could even have gone to Yelden Hall, if you hadn't sold it!'

He caught hold of her by the shoulders and shook her hard, his face a mask of fury. When eventually he released her, she almost fell. 'You have no idea, have you? No idea at all!'

*   *   *

'I cannot explain it,' Dora said to her sister the following day, as they were both sitting in the nursery, admiring baby Charles. 'I know Mrs Maxfield has been very kind and obliging and hospitable, but I do not like the woman, and I do not want to go to her house. I know that she is Bev's cousin, but I cannot help the way I feel.'

'I do not like her either,' replied Fenella. 'I think it is because she is always so full of enthusiasm.'

'But you are full of enthusiasm as well, Nella,' replied Dora.

'Yes, I know, but Mrs Maxfield has enough for two, and she seems to take all of mine away.'

Dora laughed, but not in quite the bright, open way, that she had always done when they were at home in Berkshire. 'I suppose that you are worse off than I,' she said reflectively. 'You will actually be related to her by marriage, whereas I . . .' She was silent for a long time.

'Nella, I sometimes wonder whether Charlie is so in love with London life and all his new London friends that he does not want my company at all.'

'Dora, how can you talk in that way?' exclaimed Fenella. 'He cannot possibly feel such a thing! Why, you have just presented him with a splendid son and heir.'

Dora smiled down at her baby, fast asleep in his cradle. 'He is the most adorable baby, isn't he?' she said.

'Of course he is,' replied Fenella. 'And don't forget that in addition, you are by far the most beautiful woman for miles around. Half the men in London are at your feet.'

'Nonsense!' exclaimed Dora, flushing a little. Fenella's encouraging words were not without effect, however, for a few minutes later, she said, 'Doctor Driver has said that I may go out now. Shall we order the carriage and go for an airing?'

Fenella readily agreed, and they both went to prepare for the outing. No sooner had they come downstairs, and before the order had been given, than the door opened to admit Mr Grindle and Mr Beville. It was only the second time that Fenella had seen Bev since he had left the cottage, the first time being when he had visited Dora and her new baby with his cousin. She recalled how he had said that it might be wise for there to be a little distance between them for a time. It was only now she saw him again that she realized how much she had missed him.

Both he and Mr Grindle looked well turned out, Simon in a green coat, and Bev in blue. In Fenella's eyes, though, Bev appeared the more elegant of the two.

Simon made his bow, then presented Dora with an enormous bunch of golden roses. 'I have no need to ask you how you are,' he said gallantly, 'for I can see that you are blooming.' She smiled at his compliment, but the increase in her pleasure when he enquired about the baby was quite plain.

Whilst they were talking, Bev took Fenella's hand and raised it to his lips. 'I've missed you,' he said. She said nothing, but her eyes, raised to his face, told him that she felt the same. Somehow at that moment all her suspicions seemed unimportant when set beside the happiness of seeing him again.

'We have come to see whether you are allowed to drive out, and whether we might have the pleasure of accompanying you,' said Simon.

'You must have read our minds,' declared Dora. 'I have just been told today that I am now allowed outside, and we were about to do that very thing, were we not, Nella?'

'Then may we come, or is this a ladies only event?' Bev asked.

'How absurd!' replied Dora. 'Of course it is not! We should be delighted to have your escort.'

The day was fine and mild, and Fenella reflected that it was very agreeable to travel through the streets to the park in such an elegant equipage and with two handsome male escorts. Simon and Bev appeared to have struck up a friendship with one another, and their lively conversation kept the ladies very well amused.

There were plenty of other people taking the air in the park that day, and quite a number of them were kind enough to enquire about Dora's health and that of her baby. To all of these enquiries, Dora responded with pleasure. Motherhood appeared to have given her an added glow, and Fenella was conscious that both the gentlemen sitting opposite found much to admire in her lovely sister. It was not an unprecedented situation: as soon as they had been old enough to attend social functions, Dora had always been the main attraction, with Fenella being the one to whom men had felt bound to be pleasant because she might be a means of access to her beautiful older sister. She had also sometimes acted as a confidante for those who felt that they stood no chance with Dora. This had never worried Fenella, because Dora was utterly without personal vanity, and had considered herself bound to Charlie for as long as anyone could remember. Now, however, as she kept seeing Bev's gaze return to her sister, she was conscious of a very unfamiliar feeling that she would rather like to push Dora out of the carriage altogether so that she might have Bev to herself.

Much to her annoyance, it was Bev who said eventually, 'Lady Yelden, are you tiring? Would you like to return now?' Fenella glared at him. She had quite forgotten that as host, it would be entirely appropriate for him to keep a watchful eye on the needs of his guests.

Dora smiled at his thoughtfulness. 'Thank you, yes, I think that I have been out long enough for my first time,' she said.

Bev gave the order for the barouche to return home. It was at this point that Charlie's curricle came into view. Charlie was driving his favourite pair of chestnut horses, and seated next to him on the box, in a dashing cherry red carriage dress, was Mrs Maxfield. They both looked very well satisfied with each other's company.

Fenella heard her sister take in a sharp breath and look away, but it was of no use. Connie Maxfield had pointed them out, and although Charlie looked somewhat reluctant, he guided his pair over so that he could pull up next to them.

'Good day to you all!' exclaimed Mrs Maxfield. 'You have a charming family party there, Bev. You look quite the patriarch!'

'It's not really my role,' he replied pleasantly, but his smile faded as he turned to look at Charlie. Charlie's hands tightened on the reins and the horses bridled a little.

'You see I have a fine place here,' Mrs Maxfield went on. 'Lady Yelden, you cannot believe how dull I was! But thank goodness your husband took pity on me, and has brought me out for a drive. Is that not kind of him?'

'Very kind,' said Dora colourlessly.

'It is a lovely day, is it not?' went on Charlie's companion.

'It is indeed,' agreed Fenella, more in order to save her sister from speaking than from any desire to have conversation with the woman. 'This is Dora's first outing since the baby was born.'

'Then it is fortunate that you picked such a pleasant day,' replied Mrs Maxfield.

'We are doubly fortunate to have been the ones to escort Lady Yelden on her first outing,' said Simon smiling, but his smile had an edge to it. In the glance that he threw at Charlie, Fenella was reminded slightly of the way in which he had looked at Dora's necklace, and found it wanting.

Charlie's horses bridled again, and he said tersely, 'Come, we must continue. I shall see you later, no doubt . . .'

The conversation, as they returned, lacked the lively quality that it had had before, and although the gentlemen came in when they all reached Curzon Street, they did not stay for long.

'I am sure that you are longing to rest,' Simon said to Dora, the kindness in his voice almost bringing tears to her eyes.

'Yes, I think I will lie down for a little while,' she answered. The sparkle with which she had started their outing had now quite gone, and she went upstairs as the gentlemen were leaving.

Charlie returned to the house a little later after Dora had had her rest. She and Fenella were together in the saloon. He came into the room and, without any preamble, upbraided her for her lack of courtesy. 'Connie was perfectly willing to converse with you today, and all you could come out with were sulky monosyllables!'

'I wasn't feeling very talkative,' Dora replied, turning a little pale at this sudden attack.

'When I think of the gracious invitation that she has extended to you as well! And you did not even mention it! I do not know what she must think of your manners.'

'I'm sure I do not care in the least what she thinks,' Dora retorted, recovering her equilibrium. 'I have no interest in her, or in her opinions.'

'She has offered you her friendship—'

'No, Charlie, she has offered *you* her friendship.'

There was a brief silence, after which

Charlie, who had turned a little pale, said, 'And what is that supposed to mean?'

'It means that I desire neither her friendship nor her hospitality,' replied Dora, standing firm.

'Well, that is very unfortunate, for I have accepted her invitation to Cliff House on your behalf,' said Charlie, almost shouting. 'Let that be an end of it.'

Fenella had felt a very unwelcome third during the conversation and, as the door closed forcefully behind Charlie, she could not think of anything to say to her sister that might soothe her or make things better.

In the event, after sitting in silence for a short time, Dora changed the subject completely by saying, 'I've been thinking, Nella, that I ought to start going out again in the evenings. If I accept some invitations, then I will see more people, and that will make me feel more cheerful. After all, we had a happy outing in the park today, didn't we?'

Fenella immediately felt an upsurge of jealousy at the recollection of how Bev had looked at Dora, but she repressed it at once. To maintain her sister's mood of optimism was the most important thing at present. 'Yes, we did,' she replied. 'Do you want to go out tonight, or are you still tired from your outing?'

'I am not at all tired,' answered Dora. 'Let's go out tonight, but let it be to something quite sedate.'

Fenella went over to the mantelpiece to pick up the invitations that were lying there. 'There is a musical evening at the home of Mrs Barnet. That should not be too taxing.'

'That sounds the very thing,' replied Dora. 'Why not send a message to Dudley and Augusta to see whether they are going as well? Then we can go together as a family party.'

Dudley and Augusta had indeed planned to go and they willingly agreed to take up Dora and Fenella in their carriage. They made a merry group, for Dora had clearly resolved to put her disagreements with Charlie behind her. For his part, Dudley had now ceased to look at Dora with a wistful expression. It was rumoured that he had been seen more and more frequently in company with Miss Maxfield, and it seemed that his infatuation with Dora was over.

'You look much happier,' Fenella said quietly to her sister, as they arrived at Mrs Barnet's house, and then she felt that she could have kicked herself for reminding her of what had happened earlier.

Dora took her comment quite calmly, however, and merely said, 'Yes, I am. If Charlie can be fashionable and flirt, then so can I! He's not going to have the satisfaction of seeing me mope at home.'

While applauding this resolve in general, Fenella could not help hoping that Dora would resist flirting with Bev. Her own relationship with him was on far too shaky ground for it to withstand this fresh onslaught very easily.

The rooms were already well filled when they arrived, and although Dora had met a good many people in the park, there were plenty of others who had not seen her since her confinement and who were anxious to congratulate her on the birth of a son and heir. Among them was Lord Appleby, who also continued to be attentive to Augusta.

It was while the two sisters were sitting together, taking a welcome rest from the busyness of the evening, that they heard two women talking behind a pillar quite close to them.

'I cannot understand it,' one of them was saying. 'His wife is twice as beautiful as she is.'

'Do you think she knows?' asked the other.

'No, she's one of those sweetly naive girls from the country—more fool her.'

'Of course, the affair was going on even before they were married. Once Connie has got her claws in . . .'

'Well, he always was susceptible,' replied the first. 'But you would have thought that he would be more attentive to his wife, especially after she has just presented him with an heir.'

'There's men for you,' was the answer; then the voices faded as the speakers moved away.

Fenella looked at her sister and saw that her face was quite white. 'Dora, my dear, it might

239

not have been . . .' she began.

'Oh Nella, of course it was,' said Dora in a tight little voice. 'Don't try to protect me: I'd been suspecting it for ages.'

'Dora, no,' protested Fenella. 'He loves you . . .'

'Once he did,' her sister replied wearily. 'But you've seen how fashionable he's become. He outgrew his love for me a long time ago. If I hadn't flirted with Bev at that ball in Cookham, I don't believe he would ever have turned to me again.'

Fenella was too horrified by this statement to make any response to it. Later, she would admit her own responsibility, but not now. Instead, she said, 'You can't go to stay at her house now.'

'No, I can't. I shan't do it, and if he protests, I'll tell him why.'

'Do you want to go home?' Fenella asked her.

Dora shook her head. 'No, not yet. I should only sit and brood. What I need is something to take my mind off this. Will you find someone to talk to me, please? Someone who will talk and talk and not expect too many answers?'

Seated not very far away from them was old Lady Larson, famed for her ability to keep anyone from getting a word in edgeways, and it was to her that Fenella led her sister.

'I'll send someone to rescue you later,' she

240

promised.

She turned round and at that moment, saw Bev walking towards her. Because his appearance caught her unawares, she said to him a trifle too loudly, 'Did you know that your cousin was Charlie's mistress?'

Bev looked thunderstruck, but instead of answering her immediately, he caught hold of her arm. 'For God's sake, have more discretion in a public place,' he hissed, then pulled her into an ante-room and closed the door. 'Say that again,' he said, when they were both inside.

'Did you know that your cousin was Charlie's mistress?' she repeated.

He walked away from the door, not speaking for a moment or two, then he said, 'I had my suspicions.'

'You had your suspicions? Why didn't you say something?'

'To whom?' he asked her.

'To me,' she suggested.

'Oh really? And during what kind of conversation do you think that would have been an appropriate subject for me to raise?' he asked her, his tone sarcastic.

'Never mind appropriate,' she flashed back at him. 'My sister has just discovered it through overhearing a conversation in there. Exactly how appropriate do you think that experience was?' In her anger, she had momentarily forgotten that Dora had said that she had already suspected it.

'I am sorry that she should have discovered it in such a way, but how would my telling you have changed things? Are you seriously telling me that you would have informed her if you had learned of my suspicions?'

Angry as she was, Fenella thought about how she had known of Charlie's intention to sell Yelden Hall, but had said nothing to her sister. 'Perhaps not,' she agreed. 'But if you have had your suspicions, why did you not put a stop to it?'

'And how do you think I might have done that?' He was standing, his hands in his pockets, his shoulders propped up against the mantelpiece. His hair was powdered tonight, his coat of midnight blue fitted him superbly, and altogether he looked the complete man of fashion.

'By warning your cousin off; or by telling her husband so that he could do so.'

'Stephen does not care two straws what she does, so long as she does not interfere with his pursuits. As for speaking to her myself, I can assure you that that would be of no use. Connie would never listen to me. She is extremely tenacious of purpose, and what she wants she takes.'

At once, Fenella remembered one of the women whom she had overheard saying that Connie had 'got her claws' into Charlie. She stared at Bev. 'You must have known that

242

about her when you first met me and I asked you to flirt with Dora,' she said.

'Yes, but—'

'Apparently, Charlie and your cousin were lovers even before Charlie married Dora.'

'I couldn't say.'

'A likely story,' sneered Fenella. 'You knew all along what was happening, but you said nothing so that your cousin could get what she wanted. And, in the meantime, you could get what you wanted as well!'

'Which is . . . ?' he asked her, suddenly still.

'Don't think I haven't noticed you looking at Dora,' she stormed. 'And to think I started it all off by asking you to flirt with her! I suppose you imagine that if your cousin takes Charlie away, then Dora will turn from him to you, but you couldn't be more mistaken. My sister holds marriage in much higher regard than you and your cousin appear to do. Kindly consider our engagement at an end. I have no desire to be married to a man whom I cannot respect. Now, if you will excuse me, I will go to my sister.'

She walked over to the door, but anticipating her move, he crossed the room in swift strides and blocked her way.

'Kindly allow me to pass,' she said coldly.

'Oh yes, that would suit you, wouldn't it? But you have had your say; now you will allow me to have mine.'

She opened her mouth to speak, but he

said, 'Be silent, or I'll gag you. I didn't know anything about any relationship between Charlie and Connie before I came to London. Yes, I knew Connie's character, but recall that when you and I first met, I had only just returned from abroad.

'Yes, I have suspected for a little while that there was something going on between them, but I repeat, what was I to do? You, I think, would have hesitated to say anything to your sister on such a delicate matter. It was certainly not my place to tell her, and from my experience of Connie, the only notice that she would take of me would be to go even more tenaciously for what she wanted.'

He paused briefly. 'All of your accusations in this matter I find distressing, but comprehensible.' He took a deep breath. 'However, your belief that I am infatuated with Dora, and will, it appears, go to any lengths to secure her favours I find incomprehensible and disgusting. I think that I probably respect Lady Yelden as much as any woman I know. I admire her courage, her cheerfulness and her loyalty. I was looking forward to being related to her, and I could quite easily have called Charlie out on a number of occasions for the way in which he has slighted her. I would have been quite happy to explain all this to you, but you're never interested in the facts of the situation, are you? Only in ringing a peal over me. You, Miss Fenella Parrish—you, and not your sister—attracted me from the first moment I saw you. But I have very serious doubts about the wisdom of being engaged to someone who is prepared to think the worst of me on every possible occasion. I will therefore accept your dismissal—for now.

'Two things I will do, however. The first is that I'll seek Charlie out, and tell him what Dora has learned. It might be that I'll be able to talk some sense into him. But the second, my dear, is that I will kiss you goodbye.'

He remained leaning against the door and pulled her into his arms. For a moment, he stood looking down at her, his eyes glittering through half-closed lids, and then he kissed her hard on her mouth, a fierce kiss that was intended to punish her for her lack of faith in him. Eventually he lifted his head, and looked down at her. Part of him knew that the simplest course of action would be to walk away from her now and to leave, perhaps for the Continent again, and forget about her and her family's troubles. As he looked down into her face, her complexion pale, her expression anxious, almost stricken, he knew that he could not do it, and he bent his head and once more covered her mouth with his. This time, his kiss was deliberately sensual, almost defying her to resist him; and she could not, she knew that she could not any more than she could fly. At last, he released her and when he let her go, she was trembling.

As he moved away from the door, he said, 'You and I, my love, were meant to be together, and you know it as well as I. The sooner this whole sorry business is over the better, for then, perhaps, you will be able to admit that you want me as much as I want you.'

She hurried from the room, not allowing herself to think about what had just transpired. Dora needed her now and she must go to her aid. Later, there would be time for her to think about Bev, their broken engagement, and about what to do with the rest of her life.

On her arrival back at Dora's side, she found that quite unprompted, Simon Grindle had rescued her from Lady Larson, and was now hovering protectively over her.

'I think that perhaps your sister has over-exerted herself a little for a first evening outing. May I have the honour of escorting you home?'

'Thank you, that is very kind,' said Fenella. 'We should like that, should we not, Dora?'

Dora smiled wanly. 'Yes, I should. But I do not want to tear either of you away.'

Simon waved his hand dismissively. 'Do not think anything of it,' he said. 'I am ready to leave now.' He dropped his voice. 'Much more of that caterwauling and I should be fit for bedlam anyway.'

The two ladies laughed dutifully, but in all honesty, neither of them looked very cheerful.

After they had parted from Simon, Fenella debated inwardly whether or not to tell Dora that Bev was going to speak to Charlie, but eventually decided against it. After all, there was no guarantee that it would do any good, and it might even get Dora's hopes up for nothing. She could do without further disappointments.

That decision made, Fenella resigned herself to spend at least the first part of the night going over in her mind what, apart from Bev's final kiss, had probably been one of the most unpleasant evenings that she had ever spent.

CHAPTER EIGHTEEN

Bev, walking from the Barnets' house in Berkeley Square, was coming to much the same conclusion. Furthermore, he found that he had no great liking for the task that he had set himself. His acquaintance with Charlie was of comparatively recent date, and, if he was frank, he did not care for him very much. Had it not been for Fenella, he would not have bothered about the young man at all.

Briefly, he stopped in his tracks. Had it really come to this; the Wild Marauder should undertake an errand to impress a lady, almost like a knight in one of the ancient tales of chivalry? He laughed, shaking his head derisively.

As he walked on, however, he knew that that was not the whole truth of the matter. He did admire Dora, as he had said, and her plight aroused his protective instinct. He could not be indifferent to her fate after he had held her newborn baby in his arms. Even had Fenella not been involved, he must have helped Dora if he could.

Except, of course, that had he not known Fenella, he would have had no idea of what was happening to Dora. He glanced at the doors past which he was walking. How much misery lurked behind them, unsuspected by anyone outside?

Shaking off this mood of abstraction, he realized that he had nearly arrived at White's. Charlie was seldom seen there, but one of those who were present might have seen him, and it was as good a place to start as any.

No sooner had he entered the club, than he was hailed by Lord Richard Byles.

'Bev! Over here! Come and join us.'

Bev accepted a glass of wine, but said, 'I mustn't stay. I have a message for Yelden which won't keep, and I wondered whether anyone here might have seen him.'

Byles shook his head. 'Not tonight,' he replied.

'Nor I,' put in the other. 'Are you sure it won't keep till tomorrow?'

'I think not,' replied Bev gravely, putting his glass down. 'Excuse me.'

After a few more enquiries, he found someone who had seen Charlie in Slaughter's coffee-house, and soon afterwards, he made his farewells.

At Slaughter's, it did not seem at first as if he would meet with any better success. As he was about to leave, however, he was accosted by an acquaintance who was coming in at the same time.

'Evening, Bev,' he said jovially. 'Never say you're leaving.'

'I'm afraid I must. I don't suppose *you've* seen Yelden, have you, Stancliffe?'

'Haven't seen him, but I know where he's gone,' replied Stancliffe. 'Jolyon said that he was joining Yelden and some others at Haverson's.'

Bev almost blenched visibly. 'He's gone to Haverson's? With Jolyon?'

The other nodded. 'Shouldn't have thought he was well-heeled enough to game in that company, myself,' he replied.

'He isn't,' said Bev, shortly, and set off for Conduit Street, his pace quicker than before. Jolyon was a man some twenty years Charlie's senior, with a reputation for ruthlessness at the card table. There had never been any question that he was dishonest, but he was not good company for a young man of limited means. Haverson's, too, was not a desirable destination, being one of the newer hells where men played very deep.

The club was crowded when Bev arrived, and he soon noticed that several men were gathered around one of the tables, watching the play in progress. Jolyon held the bank, and from the gentle smile on his rather thin-featured face, Bev gathered that the luck was going his way. Charlie was among those seated at the table. He had put his coat on inside out for luck, but from the evidence of the dwindling pile at his elbow, this stratagem had not done him very much good. His face was flushed, his wig was slightly askew and his eyes glittered feverishly.

It was clearly too late for Bev to intervene. All he could do was watch helplessly and be ready to pick up the pieces. As he stood watching, he felt a gentle tap on his shoulder, and turning, he saw Simon Grindle standing behind him. On his face was an expression of grave concern.

'Did you know that he was coming here?' Bev asked him in an undertone.

Simon shook his head. 'I took the ladies home a short time ago. On my way back, I met an acquaintance who invited me to come here, but it's not my idea of amusement.'

A man got up from the table. 'Do you want my place, Bev?' he asked.

'No, I thank you,' Bev replied. 'I'm not staying long.'

The man looked Simon up and down. 'No need to ask if you're playing tonight, Grindle,' he sneered. 'This is a gentleman's game.'

Bev caught hold of his arm in a vice-like grip. He glanced over at Charlie. 'In whose shoes would you rather be?' he asked the man in an undertone.

'Steady on, Bev,' he replied, trying to laugh it off. 'I was only jesting, you know. Let go, won't you?'

Bev released him, but said softly, in an icy tone, 'Just so, but I think that my friend did not appreciate your . . . humour.'

'My apologies, Grindle,' said the other man nervously. 'Must've mistaken you for someone else.'

'Easily done,' replied Simon, in a tone of cool courtesy. 'You won't do it again, I dare say.' After the other man had gone, he said to Bev, 'You're a dangerous man.'

Bev said nothing, but simply raised his brows.

At last, the final card was laid, and Charlie threw himself back in his chair.

'That's it,' he said. 'I'm finished.' He picked up the glass in front of him and eyed its contents with a queer little smile. 'I've had devilish luck tonight, but I suspect it's your fault, Jolyon. That coat of yours must be the most unseemly garment I've ever seen.'

'Go home, Yelden, you're drunk,' said Jolyon, still smiling as he picked up his winnings.

'Devil take me if I will,' replied Charlie. 'At least not yet. Do you know why I hate that coat of yours so much, Jolyon? Because it was bought with money won from idiots like me. That coat of yours is covered with blood.'

'I said, go home,' Jolyon repeated. His smile had become a trifle thin, but Charlie's had widened.

'It seems that you do not understand how deeply that coat offends me; perhaps I had better demonstrate that fact to you more clearly.'

'Charlie, no!' exclaimed Bev, starting forward.

'Bev! You here?' said Charlie. 'You're just in time to see Jolyon's coat get its just deserts.' So saying, he leaned forward and dashed his full glass of wine into Jolyon's face, so that it dripped on to his collar and over his coat.

Jolyon took out his handkerchief and wiped his face carefully. Then, in his usual measured tones, he said, 'Name your friends, my lord.'

'Bev?' said Charlie.

'Don't be an idiot, Charlie,' Bev replied impatiently.

'The deed's done now,' Charlie answered, seeming almost calm and relaxed now. 'If not you, then I'll ask some other fellow, but my mind's made up.'

'Very well,' sighed Bev. 'If you will make an idiot of yourself.'

Jolyon turned to an army officer standing nearby. 'Bentinck, you'll act for me?' The officer nodded.

'Where and when?' Bev asked Charlie.

'We'll settle it here and now,' he replied, with the same smile. 'I've a fancy to get it over and done with.'

'Don't be a fool,' urged Bev. 'Wait till morning at least. We'll go to Chalk Farm and have it out in the proper way.'

'No,' replied Charlie. 'If I wait, that coat will continue to offend me and I shan't sleep a wink all night. Let it be now.'

Jolyon broke in at this point. 'I'm agreeable. Why eat into another day's gaming when we can settle this business immediately? Are we fighting with swords or pistols, Yelden?'

'We each have a sword,' answered Charlie as he stripped off his coat. 'Why bother with any other weapon?'

'Agreed,' replied Jolyon, also removing his coat.

By now, Haverson himself had been alerted to what was afoot and he hurried over, his rather lugubrious face looking even more unhappy than usual. 'Mr Jolyon, sir! My lord! Pray, wait to the morning when you are cooler, and duel in some other place! You will ruin me with this madness!'

'Nonsense,' replied Jolyon impassively. 'All of London will flock here to see where blood was spilt!'

Haverson turned to Bev. 'Mr Beville! I beg you, exert your influence to stop them.'

'I've tried,' answered Bev. 'And so has Mr Bentinck.' He added under his breath, 'And to think they called *me* the Wild Marauder!'

In the meantime, the gentlemen present, seeing what was afoot, had begun to move furniture out of the way, and Bev made one last attempt to turn Charlie from his purpose. 'Charlie, think of Dora,' he said urgently.

Charlie looked directly at him, and for an instant, in his eyes, Bev saw the country boy that he had once been. 'I am thinking of her,' he said. Then he summoned one of the waiters and called for pen and paper.

Bev turned to Bentinck, who was standing with Simon. 'This is a sorry business,' he said.

Bentinck nodded. 'Most irregular,' he agreed 'But they are clearly determined upon it.'

'This is appalling,' uttered Simon, unable to keep silent any more. 'If anything happens, who is to tell Lady Yelden?'

'We'll cross that bridge when we come to it,' Bev replied. 'Meanwhile, we must make sure that all's as fair and proper as it can be. Simon, will you get rid of all of these fellows and keep them out, whilst Bentinck and I check the swords and make sure that the light is fairly distributed?'

Haverson took a rather dim view of being

ejected from his own gaming-room, but Simon left him with no choice. 'Besides,' he pointed out, 'if you aren't in the room, then no one can blame you for what happens in it, can they?'

By the time these tasks had been performed, both combatants were ready and Charlie, using the pen and paper which the waiter had brought, had scrawled a few lines, which he said he wanted Bev and Bentinck to witness.

'What is it?' Bev asked, as he picked up the paper.

'Read it,' said Charlie. 'Read it out loud for the others.'

Bev did as he was bid.

In the event of my death, I appoint Mr Giles Beville to be executor of my estate, to act jointly with my solicitor, Mr John Soames of Soames, Soames and Poynter. I also commend my wife and son to the care of Mr Giles Beville.

He looked straight at Charlie. 'Why me?' he asked him. 'Devil take it, you don't even like me—or I you, come to that.'

'You kept my wife safe, you have held my son: I know I can trust you,' he said. 'Now watch me sign it.'

'Charlie . . .' Bev began.

'You'll do it, won't you?' asked Charlie, wrinkling his brow. 'You'll look after them?'

'Charlie, it won't come to that,' Bev protested.

'So sign it to humour me, then,' answered Charlie. Bev and Bentinck both signed. 'Now I'll rest easy,' said Charlie, when it was done. It was not an unusual thing to say, but for some reason, Bev shivered and found himself wishing that the young earl had chosen some other form of words.

'Now, gentlemen, if you're set on this, let's begin,' said Bentinck addressing the two adversaries.

Simon had his back to the door to prevent interruptions, whilst Bev stood where he could observe fair play and Bentinck took his place between the two men, ready to part their swords with his own.

'Good luck, gentlemen,' he said; then the duel began. Jolyon was the more experienced swordsman, and he fought with an economy of movement and a precision of style that showed he had been well taught. Charlie was younger and more energetic, and inclined to fight with more flair and brilliance, but Bev, watching them both critically, could not help wondering how quickly he would tire. Neither man spoke. On Jolyon's face was an expression of intense concentration whilst Charlie, by way of contrast, looked elated and almost triumphant.

After a while, the tone of the bout changed. At first it had been Charlie doing all the attacking, but now it seemed as if Jolyon had taken the measure of his opponent, and was ready to go on the attack himself. This new development did not appear to alarm Charlie at all. On the contrary, he looked more buoyant than ever, and went into the attack himself with renewed vigour. Charlie's guard appeared to be holding up well, but then Jolyon lunged forward and, in that second, it seemed to Bev as if Charlie's smile widened as he dropped his guard deliberately and allowed Jolyon's sword to enter his body.

Jolyon staggered back, his sweating face suddenly pale. 'My God!' he exclaimed, his sword falling from his hand. 'He should have blocked that easily. I never expected . . . Oh, my God,' he said again.

Charlie swayed for a moment, then crumpled and, as he fell, Bev caught him in his arms and supported him to the ground. Simon brought Charlie's coat to roll up and put under his head.

'Said I'd settle . . . settle it . . . tonight,' he gasped.

'Don't try to talk,' said Bev. Then he looked up at Simon and Bentinck. 'One of you fetch a physician; the other find some cloths to staunch the flow.'

'Too late,' interposed Charlie, coughing. 'Much too late. Bev, listen. Yelden Hall's gone . . . Nothing left . . . You look after . . . after . . .'

'I give you my word,' answered Bev. 'Now

rest until the doctor comes. Don't try to talk.'

'Don't need . . . doctor . . .' He coughed again, this time more convulsively, and when Bev pressed his handkerchief to his mouth and brought it away, there was blood on it. 'Tell Dora . . . all my fault . . . She was the best . . . best thing . . . You'll look after her . . . and the boy . . .?' His eyes looked searchingly into Bev's.

'Yes, I'll do it, I promise you,' Bev said reassuringly.

At that, Charlie appeared to relax, and for a moment or two, his breathing came more easily. Then he frowned and in much fainter tones, he murmured, 'Bev . . . I can't see you . . .' Then he gave a last sigh and relaxed against Bev's arm as if falling asleep.

Jolyon turned away, his expression one of distress. Bev looked down at the young man in his arms, then looked up and said to Bentinck, 'You'd best get your man out of here and away quickly. Simon, help me here. I must go to Curzon Street and tell them what has happened. I want you to make arrangements for him to be brought home.'

They laid Charlie gently on the floor. 'Bev, do you think that he wanted—' Simon began, but Bev would not allow him to finish.

'I don't know,' he interrupted, 'and I don't want to know. Best not even hint at such a thing to Dora.'

Simon nodded. 'The bare facts of the matter

are bad enough.'

Bev went down on one knee next to Charlie. 'Rest easy, Charlie,' he said, as he gently closed his eyes.

CHAPTER NINETEEN

With all that had happened that evening at the Barnets' neither Fenella nor Dora could contemplate going to bed straight away when they arrived home.

'I don't know how it may be, but I find it quite impossible even to think about going to sleep,' said Dora. 'Do you think it would be very strange if we were to send for a cup of tea?'

'I don't think it would be at all strange,' answered Fenella. 'In fact, I sometimes think that some of the social events that we attend would be much more tolerable if there were more cups of tea and less glasses of wine.'

Dora smiled. 'Do you know, I have often thought exactly the same thing?' she said.

Once the tea had arrived and they were seated in the saloon, Fenella wondered whether or not to bring up the events of the evening. In the end, it was Dora who began to talk. 'I don't know why I was so shocked this evening,' she said, with only a slight tremor in her voice. 'I had already guessed that Charlie had—another interest, you know.'

'Dora . . .' Fenella began.

Dora held up her hand. 'It's all right,' she said. 'It's almost a relief to say it. Charlie changed when he came to London and I never knew it.' She paused. 'No, that's not really true. I knew it, but I didn't want to see it. We fell in love as children, but we both grew up, I suppose.'

Fenella took a deep breath. 'There is something I must tell you,' she said. Quickly, she told her sister about how she had first met Bev, and how she had asked him to flirt with her. 'So you see, it is all my fault,' she finished, tears starting to her eyes. 'If it hadn't been for my interference—'

'If it hadn't been for your interference, my dear, kind, caring sister, then it might have all turned out the same anyway. Mr Beville has a reputation for gallantry. I suspect that he might have flirted with me anyway. And if not, well, all the countryside expected me to marry Charlie. No doubt he would have conformed.'

They were both silent for a time.

'Dora, what will you do?' Fenella asked eventually.

'On one or two things I am quite decided,' Dora said firmly. 'I am not spending the summer at Cliff House. To be honest, I think that the best thing will be for all of us to go to Mama and Papa. I don't suppose that Charlie will want to go there, but it is not right that they should hear of the loss of Yelden Hall from anyone save Charlie himself. In any case, they will love seeing baby Charles, and his presence might soften their anger towards his father. But I do not see how many other plans we can make until it is known how much of the proceeds from Yelden Hall he has gambled away.' She sighed. 'This is not how I believed that my marriage would be, Nella,' she confessed sadly.

They sat silently for a few moments drinking their tea. Fenella could not imagine her father being anything other than furiously angry with Charlie. A careful and prudent squire himself, the idea of anyone squandering away his patrimony would be utterly repugnant to him. It occurred to her that Sir Humphrey might even be angry enough to welcome his daughter and grandson whilst forbidding his son-in-law the house. In those circumstances, would Charlie go to Cliff House alone? It did not bear thinking about.

Suddenly, Dora broke into Fenella's thoughts, startling her by saying, 'Didn't I see Mr Beville tonight at the Barnets'?'

Immediately, Fenella could feel the hot colour flooding her face, and she stammered, 'I don't know . . . Yes, I suppose . . . He was there.'

Dora looked at her reproachfully. 'Nella, you've quarrelled with him, haven't you?'

'And if I have, he deserved it,' she retorted.

She opened her mouth to disclose Bev's sins, but remembered that both of them involved Charlie's misdemeanours, and she shut it again.

'Nella, he can't help it that Mrs Maxfield is his cousin,' Dora said gently.

Fenella stared at her. 'How did you know?' she asked, too surprised for concealment.

Dora smiled. 'My dear, you are so fiercely loyal to me: don't think that I am unappreciative of it. But pray remember that each person chooses his own course of action. You blame Bev for his cousin's behaviour, but how would you have liked it if someone had blamed me for allowing you to go to Ranelagh that night?'

'It wouldn't have been fair,' replied Fenella hotly. 'You knew nothing about it.'

'Precisely,' Dora responded.

'But Dora, you said yourself that he had a reputation for gallantry,' said Fenella.

'He certainly had that reputation; but does it not occur to you that he has been doing everything possible to live that reputation down, particularly since he met you?'

'Not in every way,' answered Fenella, thinking of his gambling and his association with actresses.

For a time they sat in silence, then by mutual unspoken consent they began to talk of this and that. Much of the conversation concerned baby Charles, the remarkable progress that he had made so far, and what plans might be made for his future education. Both ladies were reaching the point when they were beginning to think about their beds with more charity, when quite unexpectedly, there was a knock on the door.

'Perhaps Charlie has forgotten his key,' Dora said. 'It wouldn't be the first time.'

Moments later, the door was opened and Bev was announced. Fenella sprang to her feet, remembering the quarrel that they had had earlier. For one absurd moment, she wondered whether he had come to pursue it further.

'Mr Beville,' Dora exclaimed. 'This is a surprise, although a pleasant one. But is it not a little late for a social call? I am afraid that I cannot leave my sister alone with you at this hour.'

He looked grave. Crossing the room, he approached her chair, went down on one knee before her and took hold of her hand. 'This is not a social call,' he said. 'Nor have I come to see your sister, although I am glad to find that she is with you. Lady Yelden, I fear that I bring tidings of the very gravest kind.'

Dora turned a little pale, and her hand went to her throat. Fenella went to stand behind her chair and put a hand on her shoulder. 'The gravest kind?' Dora repeated. 'What mean you, sir?'

'I come from Haverson's gaming-house,' he

said. He carefully avoided using the word 'hell'. 'There was a dispute over a trifling matter and Lord Yelden issued a challenge.'

'There is to be a duel!' exclaimed Dora, making as if to stand. 'He must not fight! It must be stopped!'

'A duel!' Fenella echoed. At once, she remembered how Bev had said that he had wanted to call Charlie out for his treatment of Dora. She also remembered how that very evening after their quarrel he had promised to look for Charlie. Was Bev going to fight with him?

Gently, Bev prevented Dora from rising. 'No, my lady,' he said. 'It is too late, I am afraid. The duel has already taken place.'

There was a long silence, and Dora said eventually in a voice that was deathly calm, 'Mr Beville, pray tell me: is my husband—dead?'

Bev looked down at her hand, then back up at her face. 'I'm afraid so,' he said. Fenella looked down at him, and for the first time, she saw that there was blood on his coat. He became aware of her gaze, glanced down at himself, then looked up at her.

'That's Charlie's blood,' she said. He nodded. 'You killed Charlie,' she whispered.

He stood up then. 'What did you say?' he asked, astonished.

'You killed Charlie. You went to find him—to talk to him, you said. What happened, Bev?

Was talking suddenly not enough to get some sense into him?'

'You don't really believe that, do you?' he said quietly.

'You have his blood on your coat.'

He stared at her for a moment longer, then looked down at Dora again. 'Lady Yelden, they will be bringing Charlie home very soon, now. May I suggest that you have at least some of the household roused and informed of what has occurred?'

'Yes . . . yes, of course,' replied Dora. She made as if to stand up, but then, finding herself unable to do so, she looked up at him and said, 'How stupid of me. I don't seem to be able to . . . I don't suppose you would . . . ?'

'Of course,' he answered, going over to ring the bell.

Fenella watched his progress, then came round to the front of her sister's chair to kneel down in the spot that he had just vacated. 'Dora, don't you see? Don't you realize?'

Dora looked down at her sister with a puzzled expression on her face. 'Don't be silly, Nella,' she said. 'Of course Mr Beville did not kill Charlie. You cannot possibly think that he did.'

Bev turned to look at them. His face was very pale. 'Thank you, my lady,' he said, bowing slightly. 'I'm glad that *someone* here has faith in me.'

'I have seen you hold my baby in your arms,'

Dora replied simply. 'You could never have killed my . . . my husband.' As if by saying the words, she had at last enabled herself to take in what had happened, her face crumpled, her voice broke on a sob, and Fenella quickly got up and took her sister in her arms. Moments later, the butler entered the room and Bev ushered him out. Fenella heard him telling the butler to fetch the housekeeper, my lord's valet and my lady's abigail.

As she comforted her sister, Fenella became aware of Bev quietly taking control of the whole situation. Suddenly her world, which for some reason had skewed wildly out of joint, she could not remember precisely when, miraculously righted itself. Dora had known with such certainty that Bev could not have killed Charlie. Now two thoughts came to her almost simultaneously: the first was one of amazement that she could ever have thought for one moment that he could be capable of such a thing. Of course Bev would never have killed Charlie, but she had accused him of it, and in the presence of another person.

The second thought, which struck her like a blow between the eyes, was that she was in love with him, and had been for some time. Even while most of her mind must now be given to her sister's needs, part of her wondered if by a supreme irony she had now finally killed his love for her by her own accusations at the very moment when she had discovered hers for him. Earlier, he had called her his love; the question now was, after what had just transpired, would he ever be able to forgive her?

*   *   *

Charlie was buried in Cookham churchyard along with his forbears. A flattering number of local people attended, including Mr and Mrs Grindle, and their son Simon. A number of Charlie's London acquaintances were also present, among them Bev, and Lord Appleby. Mr and Mrs Maxfield did not come, but it was understood that they had gone abroad for a time. It appeared that Mrs Maxfield was not in good health.

Fenella looked forward to Bev's arrival with a mixture of longing and dread. Although she had seen him since that dreadful night when he had come with news of Charlie's death, she had not really had a chance to speak to him. It was he who had made sure that Sir Humphrey and Lady Parrish were informed of what had taken place. He had also made all the arrangements for Charlie to be taken back to Cookham, and for Dora and Fenella to follow him.

Fenella knew that she must find an opportunity of speaking with him so that she could beg his pardon, but she dreaded the possibility of a rebuff. If Bev himself had any desire to speak with her, he did not betray it in any way. All his concern, all his care was given to Dora. Fenella, looking on, was conscious of a sensation of dumb misery. There could be no question that Dora would ever mourn Charlie for one moment less than was expected. Despite his many betrayals of her, her love for him had been very real, as was her grief, but although Fenella hated herself for thinking it, there was no denying the fact that the new widow looked enchanting in black. Bev, that noted connoisseur of female beauty could not but be aware of the fact. What was more likely than that Dora would turn to him after her period of mourning was over, especially since Charlie had committed his wife and child to his care?

Fenella was dreading having to tell her parents about her broken engagement at home, but in fact everyone was so caught up with the shocking news of Charlie's sudden death that her engagement was not mentioned at all. She knew that an explanation was inevitable at some point, but she was relieved that it should be postponed.

Bev arrived the day before the funeral, and naturally, it was arranged that he should stay at Brightstones. When he was admitted to the drawing-room, the whole family was present, with the exception of baby Charles, who was asleep in the nursery upstairs. He looked as elegant as ever, but it seemed to Fenella that he looked weary too, and it occurred to her that Charlie's death had probably given him a great deal to do.

'Mr Beville,' exclaimed Lady Parrish, 'How good it is to see you, even though you have come on such an errand! Fenella has been counting the hours, have you not, my dear?'

'Yes, of course,' replied Fenella, blushing furiously. She had risen to make her curtsy. Now, because it would have seemed strange to do anything else, she crossed the room to his side, and offered him her hand. He bowed over it politely, but his eyes, when he looked into hers, were cold, and she knew that she was not forgiven.

'Her eagerness for my arrival cannot possibly equal my eagerness to be here,' he answered. Fenella had forgotten that his voice was so deep. Having greeted her, he walked over to Dora, and bowed over her hand as well. 'Lady Yelden,' he said. 'I am glad to see you surrounded by your family. This is the best place for you at such a time.' This time, his voice was warm and compassionate, and lacked the cold edge that it had had when he had spoken to Fenella. Miserably, Fenella decided that she knew why he had been eager to be there; not because of her, but because of Dora.

'Thank you, you are very good,' replied Dora, smiling at him.

'How is my godson-to-be?' he asked. 'Is he

well?'

'He is growing every day,' answered Dora. 'How I wish . . .' Her voice caught on a sob, and at once her mother hurried over to her.

'Forgive me,' said Bev at once. 'I did not mean to cause you distress.'

'Of course you did not,' replied Lady Parrish, still soothing her daughter. 'Why do you not take Fenella for a walk in the gardens, Mr Beville? While you are doing that, Dora and I will fetch baby Charles from the nursery so that you can see him.'

'Very well,' replied Bev. 'My dear?' he said to Fenella, offering her his arm. Fenella laid her hand on it, and as she did so, she felt a thrill of sensation at the touch of him. Together, they left the room by the French windows, walking on to the terrace, and down the steps.

The accusations that she had thrown at him still hung in the air between them and, as the silence lengthened, the atmosphere did not improve. Eventually Fenella gathered all her courage together and spoke.

'You look tired,' she said. He glanced down at her in surprise, as if he had not expected her to say such a thing.

'This matter has cast a lot of responsibility upon me,' he admitted.

'Forgive me, but why should that be so?' she asked him.

'Charlie committed his family to my care,'

he replied. 'At least *he* trusted me, it appears.'

Fenella stopped, and turned towards him. 'Bev, I'm so sorry,' she said. 'Sorrier than I can possibly say. I never really thought that you had killed Charlie.'

He looked down at her sombrely. 'You thought it sufficiently to accuse me of it at the time,' he said.

She looked up into his face. Had there been the slightest sign of softening in his expression, she would have confessed that she had been blinded by jealousy. As it was, however, all she could say was 'I . . . I don't know why I said it. But I'm so sorry; so very sorry. Please, Bev, forgive me.'

He did smile, then, but it was a sad sort of smile, full of regret. 'Of course I forgive you,' he replied. 'But I am now prepared to accept your decision that our engagement must end. There cannot be any question of a marriage between us when there is no trust. Time and time again, you have put the worst possible construction upon my words and my deeds. Never have you even asked for my side of the story. I thought that with time, you might come to trust me, but I now believe that it can never be.'

She stared at him, remembering how he had warned that one of them might say something to the other that was beyond forgiveness: it seemed that she had been the one to speak those words. She had to try, just one last time.

'Bev,' she whispered, tears shining in her eyes. 'Bev, please—'

He shook his head. 'This much I will do,' he said. 'I'll maintain the fiction of our engagement until after I have left. Then you can start preparing your parents' minds for the fact that we are not suited.'

She turned, then, her hands over her face. She was unaware of how very near he was to catching hold of her shoulders and pulling her against him. In the event, he stepped back and said, 'I shall return to the house now, and let you have a little time alone.'

It was Simon Grindle who found her a short time later, when he walked across the park to pay his respects. He heard the sound of sobbing, and thinking that it might be Dora, he followed the sound until he came upon Fenella, sitting on a stone bench and crying as though her heart would break. He was a compassionate young man, and without hesitation, he sat down and put his arm around the drooping figure.

'Poor Fenella,' he said. 'You've had to be strong for Dora for so long, haven't you? It's not surprising that you need to give way yourself.'

He had misunderstood the reason for her tears; but she realized that what he said was the truth. She *had* had to support Dora, through the birth of Charles, through the discovery of her husband's gambling and infidelity, and through the tragedy of his death. Bev had been there, but her accusations had meant that his support had not been given to her. Within the comfort of Simon's embrace, her sobs gradually subsided, but her despair remained. She had been right in her suspicions. She loved Bev now, so very much, but any love that he had had for her had died and, what was more, she had killed it.

CHAPTER TWENTY

Both Sir Humphrey and Bev attended the funeral the following day, whilst Lady Parrish and her two daughters remained behind, Fenella reading the funeral service for the other two ladies from the prayer book.

Sir Humphrey and Lady Parrish now knew the full extent of Charlie's improvidence, but had very wisely said nothing of the matter to their daughter. It was, as the baronet had said privately to his lady, pointless to do so until the exact state of Charlie's finances should be known. That of course could be revealed only after the will was read.

It was now known generally that Charlie had sold Yelden Hall. The anger that Sir Humphrey had expressed had been extreme and very bitter, but he had already given vent to this in the presence of his lady, stamping around her bedchamber with the aid of the stick which he was still obliged to use. His lady had warned him most strictly against saying anything to Charlie's detriment during the reading of the will.

'It will do no good, my dear,' his wife had said, 'and will only cause Dora distress, and what is the point of that? Your condemnation of Charlie will not help her at all.'

'Perhaps not,' agreed Sir Humphrey. 'But, by God, my lady, I would have moved heaven and earth to have kept him away from her if I had realized how he would behave! And to think that we are obliged to have a hatchment over the doorway of this house in order to mourn for that scoundrel! A hatchment that should have been hanging at Yelden Hall, had he not thrown it away!'

'Your sentiments are very just,' replied his wife. 'But the hatchment is there to give respect to Dora's feelings, and she, and her son, must be our first consideration now. She will have enough to contend with, bringing up a child on her own, and trying to manage in the straitened circumstances to which Charlie's extravagance may well have reduced her.'

Sir Humphrey grunted. 'I suppose you are right,' he said grudgingly. 'As for living in straitened circumstances, we are not a rich family but naturally she may live with us if she chooses. Fenella will soon be married, no doubt.'

'Yes indeed,' agreed Lady Parrish. 'I do so like Mr Beville, do not you? And he is obviously so in love with her.'

'Well, no doubt you know best about such matters, my dear,' her husband replied. 'I confess I do like the man.'

'It would be better for Dora to have her own establishment,' Lady Parrish went on. 'But we shall have to wait and see whether there will be enough money for that to be possible.'

The only persons who were present for the reading of the will were Mr Soames the solicitor, Sir Humphrey and Lady Parrish, Bev, Dora and Fenella.

Before he began, Mr Soames said, 'I should perhaps explain the reason for Mr Beville's presence. In a document which, though somewhat unorthodox, is perfectly legal, the late Lord Yelden has appointed Mr Beville to be a co-executor with me. He has also commended Lady Yelden and her son to his care.'

Bev said nothing, but Sir Humphrey stretched out his hand, and Mr Soames gave the baronet the piece of paper to examine. 'Hmm. Perfectly reasonable, I suppose, since he is to be part of the family,' he said.

Fenella sat with her head bent. *Yes, as Dora's new husband one day,* she thought bleakly.

No one expected there to be anything remaining after what they had heard concerning Charlie's gaming debts, so it was quite a relief when Mr Soames read out that there was a sum of money left. 'I confess that when Lord Yelden instructed me to sell Yelden Hall, I had grave misgivings; very grave misgivings. I did my utmost to persuade him not to do so, but all my arguments were to no avail. I feared that there would be very little left for you and your son, my lady.' He paused to look at Dora, took off his glasses, polished them, and put them back on his nose. 'But thankfully, it turns out that there is a substantial sum remaining.'

'How substantial?' Sir Humphrey asked compellingly.

'Oh, something in the region of fifteen thousand pounds,' replied Mr Soames. At this news, it seemed as though the whole room sighed with relief. Only Bev continued to look impassive.

Lady Parrish broke the silence. 'Are you sure Mr Soames?' she asked the solicitor.

'Quite sure, my lady. Lady Yelden will have enough to buy or rent a small property, and may then invest the remainder to give herself a respectable income.'

Fenella looked at Dora, but she just seemed bemused. She was still taking in the news of Charlie's death, and clearly she could not give her mind to anything else for any length of time. Bev continued to sit very much at his ease, listening quite impassively to the news of Dora's inheritance. Fenella wondered forlornly whether he had so much money of his own that it did not matter to him whether Dora had any or not.

Bev stayed with them for two more days. The weather seemed to have taken its cue from Dora's mood, for it rained almost continuously for those two days. Even Sir Humphrey, a man who was normally out and about in all weathers went out very little, the damp causing his newly mended bones to ache a little. Consequently, it proved to be quite impossible for Fenella to have any private time with Bev. She did not know whether to be glad or sorry. She was so afraid that what he might say would be worse than what he had already said.

The only thing that happened that gave her the smallest feeling of hope was when one day, as she was sitting in the nursery holding baby Charles, she heard the door open, and looking up, she saw that Bev had come in. He was looking down at her and on his face was an expression of great tenderness. Before either of them could say anything, however, Charles's nurse returned and the moment was lost.

At last, on the day when Bev was due to leave, the sun came out, making everything sparkle. Brightstones and its gardens looked particularly beautiful that morning. Fenella felt that it was quite out of keeping with her mood, which was bleak and desolate.

After breakfast, she walked outside with Bev to say goodbye to him, because it was expected.

'I . . . I hope that you will have a good journey back to London,' she said in a small voice.

'Thank you, I trust I shall,' he responded politely. 'At least the rain will have laid the dust.'

'That will be an advantage,' she replied forlornly.

'Pray convey my compliments to your parents,' he said, setting his foot in the stirrup.

Quickly, before she could lose her courage, she said 'When shall I see you again?'

He looked down at her, his expression unreadable. 'Before long, no doubt. With your sister's affairs to administer—'

'Oh yes, of course,' she exclaimed. 'I had forgotten that you would be running back to see Dora at the earliest opportunity!'

'Don't be ridiculous,' he replied. You know perfectly well—'

'That Dora was committed to your care— yes, I know it,' she answered him. 'She can claim your time and attention whenever she wants. Just don't expect me to like it, that's all.'

He swung himself into the saddle. 'Don't you think it's time you grew up, Fenella?' he said.

For a moment, she stared at him, her heart

in her eyes. Then she said simply, with a catch in her voice, 'I have grown up, Bev,' and, turning away, she stumbled round the side of the house.

'Fenella, wait!' he called, but she did not return. He sat looking thoughtfully in the direction in which she had gone, then turned his horse and rode down the drive.

*   *   *

There was only one place to which Fenella wanted to go at that moment, and that was the old folly. As she ran across the grass, the hem of her gown became sodden with all the rain that had fallen, but she didn't care. All she wanted to do was to reach her safe place.

The stones felt slippery as she climbed up, and one of her usual footholds had moved a little, but she managed to climb up to her vantage point. This was where she had been when she had first seen Bev. Then, as if she had been transported back in time, she heard the sound of horse's hooves, and Bev appeared at the gate.

'That's a fine perch you have there,' he said. That was how it had all started. His return, and the clear fact that he recalled that first meeting as well as she did made her almost crazy with hope.

In a voice that trembled a little, she said, 'Yes, I can see everything.' Not asking permission to enter this time, he leaned over, unfastened the gate, then rode into the garden and, getting off his horse, he pulled the reins over its head and left it to crop the grass.

'Aren't you afraid you'll fall?' he asked her.

She was about to say no, when suddenly, she felt a slight movement below her and heard a harsh grinding sound. The heavy rain had undermined the foundations of the folly. She did not fully realize the danger she was in until Bev said in urgent tones, 'Fenella, I can't come up and get you; there's no time. You'll have to jump and I'll catch you.'

She stared down at him. The drop looked to be at least ten feet. Whilst she was hesitating, the wall seemed to move even more, and the sound grew louder.

He looked up at her, and their eyes met and held. 'You'll have to trust me,' he said. 'Come on! Hurry!'

Hesitating no further, she pulled her skirts together and dropped down into his arms. He staggered and almost fell, but gathered himself together and put as much distance between them and the folly before its main section came crashing down with a roar, on to the place where he had just been standing.

She stared at it, her face white. 'I . . . I could have been killed,' she said.

'A blessing I was here, then,' he replied. He set her on her feet, but she clung to him.

'Bev, don't let me go,' she whispered.

'Never again,' he replied, and he lowered his head and kissed her tenderly.

When eventually he released her, she said to him, 'Why did you come back?'

He grinned wryly. 'I couldn't leave. I told myself I was a fool to be so much in love with a girl who trusted me so little, but it was no good. You had wound yourself around my heart, Miss Fenella Parrish, and I couldn't break free.'

She felt her heart leap at his words. 'It was the same for me,' she admitted. 'I'm just so sorry that I didn't trust you—more sorry than I can ever say.'

He glanced over at the folly. 'You trusted me with your life just now,' he pointed out.

'I always wanted to trust you, but you didn't always make it very easy for me,' she said a little diffidently. 'One moment, you were a weary traveller on horseback, and the next you were a polished society gentleman with all the women at your feet.'

'Poor Nella,' he said. 'I suppose it was rather confusing.'

'And then, of course, it was partly because you are called the Wild Marauder. I know I only saw you gambling with Charlie once, but I thought—I assumed—'

'Fenella, there was a time when I would have watched someone like Charlie gamble away his inheritance, telling myself that it was none of my business. But your fears and

281

anxieties made me look at things differently. When you saw me gambling with Charlie, I was attempting to limit the damage that he was doing, although I must confess with indifferent success.'

'I've been such a fool,' Fenella replied. 'And I suppose that when I saw you once carousing in the street with Charlie—'

'I was trying to persuade him to go home,' Bev put in. 'It wasn't possible for me to protect him all the time; besides, the damage was done before I ever met him, you know. Since his death I have had to look into his affairs. The estate was encumbered when he inherited it, but by the time I returned to England, his debts were such that only severe retrenchment would have solved the problem.'

'No one around here knew about Charlie's debts,' said Fenella. 'Papa would never have permitted the marriage had he known.'

'To your father, Charlie was the agreeable young man whom he had always known,' Bev answered. 'It's not surprising that he should have been more trusting with him than with a suitor unknown to him.'

'I know it was stupid of me to take my anger out on you,' she confessed, 'but I felt so helpless to do anything about it, and I suppose that you must have felt the same way. But I see now that it is of no use either of us blaming ourselves. Charlie was a grown man: he knew what he was doing.' She paused. 'And then because you are Mrs Maxfield's cousin, I convinced myself that you must know all about her and Charlie.'

He laid a finger upon her lips then. 'You must believe me when I tell you that I knew nothing definite about their affair. Oh, I had my suspicions, but you have seen my cousin. She is an extravagant social butterfly, and it is not always easy to tell upon whom her fancy has really lighted. She and I are drawn together every so often because neither of us has brothers or sisters or any other cousins, but we have never been very close.'

Fenella nodded. 'Even if you had been, you still might not have known about her and Charlie,' she pointed out. 'It was Dora who reminded me that even she and I do not know everything about each other.' She paused for a moment. 'Then you seemed to look at Dora so lovingly and admiringly.'

'That's because I do admire her,' Bev said.

'I thought that you were more interested in her than you were in me,' she admitted in a small voice. 'And I was jealous. It sounds horrible, but I think that even at the moment when you came to tell her about Charlie and I saw you kneeling at her feet . . .'

'You were jealous? Of Dora?'

She nodded. 'I know it sounds absurd, but she is so beautiful, you see, and everyone falls in love with her, and she is so sweet, so how could they help it? And now that she is a mother—' She stopped abruptly, then went on, a little awkwardly, 'You and I were supposed to be engaged, but it had come about in such an awkward manner, and you never wanted to be married to me, did you?'

He laughed and pulled her back into his arms. 'I knew that you were the girl for me from the very first moment I saw you,' he told her. 'You, and not your sister. I thought I'd made that abundantly clear, but it seemed to me that you did not feel the same. The night at Ranelagh provided me with a heaven-sent opportunity. I had the perfect reason for becoming engaged to you, and I told myself that you would learn to love me as much as I love you, my darling. But then, you seemed to draw further away from me.'

'I know I did,' confessed Fenella. 'But in the end, it wasn't you I couldn't trust—it was my own feelings.'

'And do you trust them now?' he asked her softly, his lips very close to hers.

'Oh yes,' she replied, whilst she was still able. 'I love you—for now and always!'

EPILOGUE

Mrs Giles Beville and Lady Yelden were sitting outside on the lawn which was just below the mellow Jacobean house which Bev called his home. It was to this house that he had brought his bride just over a year ago, and it was here that they spent most of their time. Although still beloved of society whenever he chose to go to London, Bev showed a distinct preference for country life, and Fenella was happy to be wherever he was.

Bev's house was situated in Buckinghamshire, within easy travelling distance of Brightstones, but not so close that Sir Humphrey and Lady Parrish could live in their pockets.

Dora's parents had hoped that she would find a property very near them, but she elected to go to Buckinghamshire also, where she had found a delightful house for sale. It was much smaller than Yelden Hall, or even Brightstones, but it was big enough for herself and Charles, who was now growing apace.

Her house was close enough for the sisters to be able to see one another every day if they chose to do so, as they had always planned, and it was also close enough for Bev to be able to care for Dora and Charles, as he had promised Charlie he would.

Fenella watched as Dora played with her son. He was tottering about unsteadily on his feet, screaming with laughter if his mama pretended to chase him, and laughing even more when she caught him.

There was a time, she reflected, when she would have been jealous of Bev's interest in them. Now, secure in his love, she knew that the affection in which he held his relations by marriage was of a very different order. She changed her position in her seat, and laid a hand on her stomach. Soon, she thought, little Charles will have a cousin to play with.

A shadow crossed her face, and before he bent to kiss her, she knew that her husband had arrived.

'Good morning, my love,' he said. 'Good morning, Dora, Charles. I've brought you a pleasant surprise.'

Fenella turned in her chair to see that Simon Grindle was standing next to Bev. As he came round in front of her to greet her properly, she saw her sister glance up and blush. Dora's year of mourning was over now, and she looked very pretty in a gown of light blue. It was not long before Simon had gone to join her in playing with the baby.

'Strange how often Simon seems to find it necessary to come over here,' Bev said ironically, as he and Fenella were strolling in the gardens later.

'Yes, isn't it?' she replied demurely.

'I think they'll make a match of it,' said Bev.

'He's loved her patiently for a long time,' responded Fenella. 'I used to think that she might have married Dudley, but Dudley is now engaged to Miss Maxfield.' Miss Maxfield had surprised everyone. When her brother and sister-in-law had gone abroad following the scandal of Charlie's death, she had refused to go with them, insisting that she could remain in the care of an aunt. Her ready response to Dudley's courtship had provided the reason for her stubbornness.

'It will be strange if after everything, Charles ends up living in Yelden Hall,' Bev remarked.

'Yes it will be,' she agreed. 'But Dora would never marry Simon for such a reason. And I do not believe that Simon is at all mercenary either. But at least Dora will not go to him empty handed, as perhaps we once feared.' Bev grunted, and suddenly, Fenella realized something for the first time. 'Bev, Charlie commended Dora and Charles to your care.'

'Yes, he did,' he agreed.

'Bev, did Charlie leave nothing but debts?'

'Why do you ask?' he said cautiously.

'I'm just wondering where the fifteen thousand pounds came from,' she murmured.

'Does it matter?' he asked her, raising one brow quizzically.

'No, it doesn't matter—but I think you're wonderful,' she said, smiling up at him.

'The feeling, my dearest wife, is entirely mutual,' he answered, as he pulled her into his arms.